MOTH
BOY

MOTH BOY

CLARE HUDMAN

The Book Guild Ltd

First published in Great Britain in 2021 by
The Book Guild Ltd
9 Priory Business Park
Wistow Road, Kibworth
Leicestershire, LE8 0RX
Freephone: 0800 999 2982
www.bookguild.co.uk
Email: info@bookguild.co.uk
Twitter: @bookguild

This work is entirely fictitious and bears no resemblance to any persons living or dead.

Typeset in 11pt Adobe Garamond Pro

Printed and bound in the UK by TJ Books LTD, Padstow, Cornwall

ISBN 978 1913913 533

British Library Cataloguing in Publication Data.
A catalogue record for this book is available from the British Library.

To all adopted and fostered
children everywhere, with love.

THE TRUNKS

When I got left in the plastic bag as a baby boy, I had no name, not even a surname. Some random social worker named me Ches and then when Mum adopted me, I got the Trunk surname. So, this is me, Ches Trunk. Very nearly at the end of my first ten years in family Trunk.

I am not a blood relative of Raffy Trunk, not even a stepbrother. But we are connected in a funny way that my brain can't untangle. We're all in the same class. Three Trunks. Yes, yes, I've heard it plenty times before – *tree* trunks. Ha, ha. Me, Raffy and his twin sister, Inga.

But there's more than that. My mum, Aggi, used to be married to his dad and wishes she still was. She even still wears her wedding ring "to keep the hordes off", she jokes. But really, it's because it wasn't her who walked out. Maybe that's why Raffy hates me, because she refuses to change her name. Whenever Michael "Sideburns" Trunk turns up for a school event Mum always remembers to put a flower in her hair and a bit of lippy on. Worse, she over-eggs the public cuddles, smothering me with mum perfume.

'I'm going to show him I'm a good mother when it counts. He missed out. We could have done this together – him and me – a team.'

I don't think I needed to know that.

According to Aunty Bella, Mum had three miscarriages, so Michael Sideburns left her for a "better model". The new Mrs Trunk produced two babies at the same time, one boy, one girl, Raffy and Inga. Mum reckons "that estate agent woman of his chose the poncy names, and it's about all the input she gave those kids".

I never said, '*Mum, she might be too busy to look after them now, but she grew them for nine months in her body. That's a big deal, isn't it? And she loves them enough to still live with them.*'

Or maybe it's that Raffy hates the way I look totally unlike a real Trunk. Perhaps he thinks my brown skin somehow rubs off on him because we're both called Trunk. I know it's weird, but people *are* weird about stuff like that. I've caught him smirking if anyone calls me coffee or toffee or something much, much worse. Although he's not actually racist to my face he's definitely enjoying my pain.

Unlike the Trunk twins I've got tight fair curls, light brown skin and a weedy body. I am no Trunk and actually neither is Mum. She's shortish and curvy with "a bit of padding for sitting comfortably". I like it how in the summer her gardening job makes her turn almost the same shade of brown as me. The real Trunks are huge, athletic and white.

Raffy isn't as popular as Inga. He's not into sport because he's too lazy. He's almost as tall as his sister and has equally thick, dark hair, but his face is pale, broad and mean-looking. He has dark eyes that are on the lookout for opportunities to put someone down and a ticklish cough thing he does even though he hasn't actually got a cough. He hangs out with Felix, who looks like he is one stop short of being an albino. His hair is unbelievably blond and very bushy. He's got grey eyes and he blinks a lot.

Those two are always skulking together around the cloakroom or the back of the class. I know they're being mean. I'd say "bitching", but Mum's banned me from using that word because it's sexist. There isn't another word I can think of.

Inga doesn't worry me at all. She's got her own world of sport and can't be bothered with Raffy's little hate campaigns. She wins all the high jump and long jump competitions and the races too. Anything she wants to do physically she has a ridiculous advantage of height over all of us. I'm so puny I don't get to be good at lots of stuff where height and weight count. I can run, though. Fast. Faster than Raffy.

Mum knows, although I haven't told her the half of it, that Raffy has got it in for me. It's hard to keep explaining why my PE kit is smeared with blackberries, or why I've got chewing gum tangled in my shoelaces. Mum can mostly tell when I'm lying. I've begged her not to do or say anything because it'll be even worse for me, if Raffy finds out I've told anyone.

'Relax. I can handle it. Relax, Mum. At least I'm in one piece.'

I've got four weeks left to keep my mum from marching around to Michael Sideburns with my ruined PE kit in her hands. I know it wouldn't end up well. Mum would get upset, have one of her headaches, and I'd end up with more venom from Raffy. It's best to ignore it. Then it'll go away. I'm going to a different school from him in September. New start. Solly, George and Sasha are all going to my new school. I'll be OK. Not much longer now.

BIRTHDAY TALK

I get back from school and the house stinks. A wall of vinegar smarts my eyes as soon as I open the door to our flat at the top of the stairs and step into the kitchen.

'Mum, open the window. We're going to axiphycate with all these fumes.'

Mum's laughing and shaking her head, 'Asixyphate, no, asph… asphyxiate. That's it, asphyxiate. What a crazy word!'

She's adding bay leaves to a steaming pan and showing no signs of opening any window, so I dump my homework bag on the table then lean over all the cooking mess to open the windows wide.

'I got a ton of shallots from old Mrs Langdon so it's pickling time. Sorry about the mess, love, and the smell. How was school? You wouldn't be a best boy and put the kettle on, would you? I'm gasping. I don't think I've had a drink since I finished with her veggie patch. There's so much to do and her hip is taking an age to mend. Oh well, at least it fills the coffers, eh? And it's only up the road.'

'Coffers? What are coffers?'

'You know, puts money in our purse. It'll pay for the uniform you'll need for September, for your new school. Thanks, love. You're a gem.'

She starts humming one of the many salsa tunes she has stored in her head and shimmies her shoulders over the chopping board scattered with dark red chillies. Tonight is her teaching salsa class and Aunty Bella is coming over to keep me company. She lifts the board and, with a theatrical slide of her knife, scrapes the wrinkle-skinned chillies into the pan then turns the heat off.

'Let's have a cuppa together, eh? I'll sit down, you sit down, and we'll have a chat through stuff.'

I'm not sure this is a good idea. I've got a bad feeling and I want to skulk off over to my room and lie out on my bed, look at the clouds drifting past the skylight window or sit at the top of the fire-escape stairs and watch the magpies hopping about. One for sorrow, two for joy, three for a girl, four for a boy.

On the small, square patch of perfect grass below is an under-used short plastic slide for the downstairs man's part-time child. It looks like an advertisement for a kid's toy in a magazine.

An old plum tree hangs over the fence from next door. There's always a bit of life in that tree. It changes over the year. First, it's a skeleton tree with blackbirds singing full throttle, standing like happy soldiers amongst the branches. In spring, pink petals float in through my window and land on the carpet. When the plums ripen at last, and the man is out at work, me and a mate are going to leg it over the fence, tiptoe over the grass and fill our pulled-out T-shirts with oodles of fat, juicy fruit.

Unlike the plum tree, the boring grass stays the boring same. The man downstairs suggested to Mum that she does her "gardening magic" (Mum's finger quotes) on his patch of grass. But she's far too busy sorting out other gardens where she actually gets paid to bother with his. Anyway, she only does old or poorly people's gardens because there's always an end in sight and space for something new that way.

Mum doesn't like the idea of being trapped in a job and I wonder if sometimes she feels that having me is a trap. She could have anyone, go anywhere, except she's got me. Does she wish she had fostered me instead and then she could have given me back? I always feel wobbly around my birthday time. Don't know why. Well, yes, I do, but it's stupid, isn't it?

'Please, lovely. Come on, sit down. Not for long and I'll let you go.'

I sit down with a sigh and feel my lips pulling together, disappearing, like Mum does with her lips when there's something she'd like to say but thinks better of it.

'About that birthday of yours coming up. Don't make a face, Ches. I know you'd like to ignore it and for the life of me I don't know why you and birthdays don't hit it off. Most kids—'

'I'm not most kids. I'm me.'

I don't say, '*I'm adopted – remember? Every birthday, every extra birthday candle leaves me less and less hope that she'll ever come and find me. Whoever she is.*'

'Yes, well, that's certainly true. You are your own person, Ches.'

She doesn't say, '*I know you're adopted, but that's no excuse. Let's forget that. I'm your mother and I'm doing my best – and all on my own.*'

We both clutch on to our mugs and stare at the milky tea

within. I'm not going to make this easy. It's not me who wants a jolly, jolly happy little birthday celebration next Sunday.

'Ches, lad, look here. I've got something to tell you and it's rather important.'

I look up because I can hear a quivering in her voice. Her silver-blue eyes dart around like miniature fish, searching me for inspiration as to how to word what she wants to say. I'm now sitting bolt upright and very still like the herons you see at the edge of the canal. I swallow loudly.

'I don't want you to build your hopes up. That's what I'm worried about. She's probably got her own life now, her own children. Your birth mother. Ches. Ches?'

This is sudden. She next to never mentions her. There's not much to talk about. Not much to go on. All I know is I was found on a doorstep in a bag and I was only just born. Tiny. Still with a raggedy bit of umbilical cord attached.

My brain catches up with what I have just heard Mum say. I want to shout out, '*Aren't I her child then? What about me?*

Instead I can feel my bottom lip curling out and I blink a lot. It's ten years since my mysterious birth mother put me on a doorstep and walked away. Of course she has her own life. A lot happens in ten years.

'It's all right, Mum. I haven't got my hopes up. I just don't really like birthdays. The cake and all the fuss. Can we just go out with Aunty Bella or something? I'd like that. No cake or candles. Please?'

'And a friend or two? What about the other boys in your class? Solly? George? Or a girl if you'd prefer. Whoever you'd like.'

'No, Mum. I'd like it just us. It's my birthday, after all.'

I don't say, '*Friends wouldn't understand how it's no fun celebrating the day you got abandoned. It reminds me I'm different.*'

I scrape my chair back, grab my school bag and run along to my room before Mum can think of something else to say and before she can see that I'm upset. I've got one of those faces that crumples into tears way more than strictly necessary. Who did I get that from, I wonder?

PIZZA

Because my mum gets so many free vegetables and fruit from her gardening jobs, we don't get to eat out much. But she's not that fond of spending time in the kitchen, cooking meals. She says that her mum, Nana Lil, never taught her to cook: 'Nana Lil was too busy going out and drinking herself silly to bother with cooking for us two girls. We were brought up on baked beans and pasta, sometimes together, if she'd forgotten to get some bread in.'

Mum is nervous in the kitchen. She tries to cover it up by singing but I can tell. When she was married, Michael did most of the cooking. Then, when she adopted me, she was determined to do something better than what she'd had as a child. She's got all these kid's cookbooks but actually they were for her. Now they're for me and I love cooking. Mum is always so grateful and full of admiration when I produce something cooked, that it's a cinch to shine in the kitchen.

Today, though, I don't feel like cooking or even helping to cook. The kitchen is a mess after her pickling fest. There's a knock on my door. I wait for a bit, thinking about what I'm going to say if she asks me to help with cooking. She knocks again and calls in a quiet voice, 'Ches? Do you fancy going out for a pizza?'

It's a no-brainer.

I love walking outside when it's still so light and warm in the evenings that you don't even have to think about wearing anything more than a T-shirt and shorts. There are literally more than twenty pizza places to go to within reasonable walking or cycling distance of our flat.

We've chosen to walk into town along the wide pavements with tree roots bursting through the tarmac, get a takeaway and go and sit in the park behind Cheltenham Town Hall. We nearly turn away and find another pizza place because of what's on the bottom but one step. It looks like orange candle wax dripping down from one step to the next.

'Was that before or after the pizza?'

'Mum, that's gross.'

'I'm kidding. They'd never make it up the steps in that state. Now if we go in here it's margheritas only, OK?'

Mum carries the big, flat cardboard boxes whilst I take a detour to hare up the sloping pathway, stride behind the grand stone pillars of the town hall and glance through the huge glass doors at the people milling within, before racing down the other side to join Mum. It's just something I like to do. Perhaps my birth mother is posh and regularly goes to venues like this. She could be a world-class opera singer or a harpist. I sometimes think she's trying to tell me to go to certain places so she can see me. Today I got too close to a door and it opened automatically. A woman sitting in the kiosk thing glanced up at me as I skirted past the other two tall doors. Nobody else was around. Not today.

Mum's brought a blanket to sit on and a mega bottle of tap water to share. There are loads of people sitting eating, drinking and chatting. Some people are lying down asleep. All the benches in the tree shade are occupied. There are a few big boys kicking a ball about so Mum chooses a place well away from them, next to a circular bed of bright pink and purple flowers.

I can't wait to eat my mozzarella and tomato pizza, all hot and gooey. Neither of us talk. We are hungry.

It doesn't take long, though, before I'm thinking that if I have one more piece I'm going to burst. That's when Mum starts talking.

'Ches. I've got something that I need to give you on Sunday. When you're ten. I've been saving it because those were the instructions. The social worker said that I could decide nearer the time, when you were older, what to do.'

My heart is thumping like crazy.

'I tried to tell you earlier. It's nothing to be worried about, I'm sure. Your birth mother left something for you to let you know a bit about herself and how she was feeling at the time.'

Monster worms are squirming in my guts.

'She wrote on the envelope that it was a present for you for when you were ten. Well, you are nearly ten and I think it's a good idea to give it to you. I think you'd be cross with me later if I didn't do it now. It's hard to know. Hard to decide. To make the best decision for you.'

This feels like we're in a film and it's not really happening.

'I just want you to read it and I'm here for you if you need to talk about it. And I think it's just what it is. Something for you to know a bit more about her. Nothing else.'

I have no idea what to say. How do you respond to that?

I feel a bit sick. I haven't had time to digest my pizza and it's feeling in danger of making another appearance. I can't help thinking about the sick on the pizza restaurant steps. I look around for a waste bin. I'm getting very overheated. And then I get up, lean over the flowerbed and cover some pink flowers in undigested pizza. Wow. I am shaking but feeling better all of a sudden. Mum is half-cuddling me, giving me a tissue and sounding worried.

'Have you finished? Do you want some water? Ches, I'm so sorry.'

'Water. I need some water.'

I rinse my mouth out and spit it onto the soil several times until my mouth is clean enough to drink. There's nothing like clear water for drinking. Then I look at the sick-covered flowers and I don't want to be here anymore with people knowing I made that mess and staring at me. Several people have moved away.

'Can we go home?'

Mum pours the rest of the water over the flowers, gathers the pizza box containing remains I'm trying not to think of and we walk back towards home. At the nearest waste bin she rams the box into its mouth, and I have to look away.

'OK, love?'

'OK, Mum.'

NANA LIL

I wasn't even one year old so of course I don't remember the first time I met Nana Lil, but apparently, she was super-curious about me.

She brought a present of an out-of-date Christmas pudding that she'd found in her cupboard. Whilst trying to hold back her huge dog from licking my face, she'd explained, 'I'll never get around to using it, Aggi, because I always spend Christmas on my own, but I'm sure you can put it to use now you've got a family to feed.'

This was a sentence that had been repeated hundreds of times by Aggi and Bella when they were trying to let anyone know what their mum was like. I mean, it was February, Mum was a single parent and I wasn't old enough to appreciate Christmas pudding. Weird or what? Mum told me that Nana Lil felt very sorry for herself and that was why she drank far too much. Her brain wasn't working properly with all the alcohol sloshing around and the regrets she kept thinking about.

I'd asked, 'What regrets?'

'She made some bad choices. Probably shouldn't have married someone who was always away working for the army. Probably shouldn't have had children – she wasn't a happy mum. And probably should have got help instead of drinking to make her forget her problems. She was a striking figure and clever and she wasted it all. She has the most amazing albums of photographs she took before she met Granpappa Dom. Mostly people. She was good at portraits and catching life in the street. All black-and-white photos. It was unusual for women to be photographers back then. And when she had kids, she had to stay at home looking after us. So, she put away her camera. It's a shame. It's different now.'

'Didn't she use it to photograph you and Aunty Bella?'

'No. It's like she couldn't bear being reminded of her past career and unfettered life. I'm so cross about that. There's very, very little of our childhood. It's not like now when anyone and everyone can snap away. Look at all the photos I've got of you growing up.'

Every time Nana Lil came to visit, Mum was on edge. Nana Lil wore plenty of jangly beads and pinky purple "fuchsia" lipstick, and she drew a wobbly black line under her eyes each morning, or whenever she got up. Her hair was long and scraped back into a ponytail. She still dyed it dark brown and there was always a grey stripe down the centre parting, sometimes thin and sometimes very wide. But what was really mad about her face were the two fat slug eyebrows above her eyes. They were ginormous and from across the room it looked like she'd stuck false ones on. Close up you could see they were real. They were wiry and wild.

On each of her visits, after we'd waved her off on the coach to London, Mum had a lot of cleaning of my bedroom to do before I was satisfied. My room always reeked of the most disgusting flowery perfume, which Nana Lil sprayed everywhere to try to disguise her cigarette smoke and spilt alcohol. The last time she stayed I could smell wafts of pongy perfume for weeks afterwards.

I had a brilliant idea for her next visit. Now I'm going to be ten I don't want to have to share a bed with Mum when Nana Lil comes. So, she can stay in Mum's room in the double bed and Mum can stay in my room and I can sleep on the sofa.

But Aunty Bella said there was no need. I can stay with her instead and then everyone gets a bed.

I asked Mum, 'Why doesn't Nana Lil stay with Aunty Bella? That'd be the simplest solution.'

'Not a good idea unless we want a murder on our hands.'

'Nana Lil's not strong enough anymore.'

'Exactly. But she's stupid enough to keep winding Bella up. It'd be a disaster. For both of them. They'd say things they regretted. No – it'll be fun staying with Bella and I promise I'll keep your room nice for you.'

I didn't say, '*What kinds of things might they say that they'd regret?*'

I knew Mum would skate around that question.

It's the day before my birthday and Mum gets a text from Nana Lil. Like – no warning at all. She is on the coach already and doesn't want to miss my birthday for anything. Can we pick her up at 16.30? That's two hours' time.

Mum's face clouds over, she shakes her head and goes to phone Aunty Bella from her bedroom.

I'm trying to think of any of my birthdays Nana Lil has ever been to before and I can't think of one. This is shaping up to be a fine old birthday. Aunty Bella, me and Mum have planned to go to the Lido in Stroud where I won't bump into anyone I know. Has Nana Lil even got a swimsuit, let alone brought it with her? And will Aunty Bella be able to stop herself from strangling Nana Lil? And will I even want to go to the Lido when I've read that letter?

AUNTY BELLA'S

Aunty Bella's hall has a neat line of footwear pushed up against the skirting board. There are four pairs of Roman sandals in brown, black, silver and bright yellow, two pairs of Doc Martens and a pair of Moroccan slippers in red leather. She dresses differently to Mum – stranger. Her hair is grey and cut very short at the back so you can see two lines of a tattoo poking up above her T-shirts. When she wears a summer vest or a swimsuit a butterfly becomes visible, drawn in black ink, placed in the centre of her spine with its wings spread out across her shoulder blades, like they are *her* wings. Its feelers are curling upwards either side of the back of her neck. And stretching up the outside of her left leg is a dandelion plant, roots and all, with a few stray seeds blowing across her calf.

Nana Lil likes to comment about Aunty Bella's tattoos. If Aunty Bella's within hearing distance it doesn't stop her.

'Why would anyone want to disfigure the skin they were born in? I don't understand. It's like she's trying to make herself look ugly.'

Aunty Bella will swear under her breath and fish out her car keys, ready to leave. She drives a Mini and I love going in her car. It's my kind of size.

After a quick courgette-heavy supper together, Aunty Bella and I say goodbye. Nana Lil squeezes my face and plants some gross pink lipstick on my nose. Mum hands an orange plastic bag to Bella that I guess has got some new item of clothing for me to put on for my birthday. My birthday is always an excuse for Mum to buy me some T-shirt or other in the next size up that she can't resist. It has its downside when it's something I'm not that keen on and I have to wear it on my birthday. I think the message is finally getting through that plain is what I like. That way she can't mess up too much.

Aunty Bella lives in a proper brick house at the end of a terrace with a hedge that she has to keep trimmed to reveal the road name sign hidden in it. She's got a slatted gate which squeaks and on her turquoise door a metal knocker in the shape of a dolphin. I follow Aunty Bella into her hall and kick my trainers off, making sure to place them to the side.

It's weird spending the night before my birthday away from Mum, but Aunty Bella is the next best thing. If I think about it, she's the only alternative. Nana Lil's ground floor flat, which I have only visited a couple of times very briefly, is kind of sad. The bathroom smells mouldy, carpets are stained from spilt drinks, and the windows hardly let any daylight in because they're so filthy. There are newspapers, books, used mugs and plates everywhere, even on the chairs, and it reeks of stale tobacco. Anyway, London's too far away.

'OK, Ches. Your last few hours of being nine? Fancy a smoothie? I've got a massive mango that's crying out to be eaten. And then I believe I've got a rematch with you. You beat me last time, didn't you? My special mini table tennis? Up for it?'

My teeth are tearing fibrous flesh off the big mango stone. I am getting in a sticky-chinned mess. I wonder why seeds are such different sizes. A ginormous cooking apple has tiny seeds and yet this mango seed is a trillion times bigger. Maybe if it's a lonely seed it has to be big to stand a chance, whereas apple pips have a whole bunch of siblings in one fruit. The apple can afford to lose a few seeds on the way. I'm just about to pipe up with this observation when Aunty Bella speaks.

'Ches. You know the letter? From your birth mum.'

My heart stops and then starts cantering.

'Mum told you.'

'Of course she did, Ches. I've known about it since you were a baby.'

I didn't say, '*So, I'm the last to know and yet it's actually mine.*'

'How are you feeling about it?'

'I don't know.'

I really don't know what to say because it changes from moment to moment. I've just felt scared, angry and humiliated in the last minute. How can I say how I'm feeling if it's a racing track of craziness? Collisions all over the place, pile-ups, flat tyres. I like this racing-track metaphor. We've been doing metaphors at school and I'm good at it. I get the point. It's not always easy to explain things. With the letter I'm hoping there will be a winner, but there's only ever one winner and that worries me. If it's me, will Mum be a loser?

'I think if I was you, I'd be feeling a whole mush of things but mostly very nervous. I don't think you need to be worried, though, Ches. Your mum is worried. Not about the letter exactly. She's worried that you'll build your hopes up too much and then feel hurt and let down. But you need to know that your mum and me – we'll not let you down. We are here for you whatever happens in your life. OK?'

I don't say, '*Not when you're both dead.*'

'OK.'

I mumble between tearing threads off the stone even though it is pretty much stripped bare now.

'Is there anything you want to say or ask, Ches?'

'Has anyone opened the letter? Already read it?'

Aunty Bella's shoulders tense and she switches on the noisy smoothie maker, giving her time to think what to say. But I've already guessed the answer. From nowhere a rage rolls through my body and before I know it, I have screamed, 'No!' and run out of the kitchen. I can't go to my room. I can't hide. I grab my trainers from the hall and run outside, pulling them on, half-hopping across the street. I don't know where I'm going. I run down the road half-hidden by parked cars, across another road then left towards the railway line. I can't hear Aunty Bella calling after me any more.

A voice is shouting inside my head: *That's private. That's mine. That's the only thing from my mother to me and they've ruined it. Nothing's fair. Nothing.*

ESCAPE

It's not quite dark yet, so a ten-year-old boy jogging along the street is totally normal, I tell myself. No one's looking at me. I haven't run away. I'm just having a breather. Or have I run away? Is this how it starts?

I need to get off the street in case Aunty Bella's red Mini comes after me. I am in one of those TV escape thrillers. My spine prickles with excitement and fear. Am I the villain or the victim? Is she the detective or the kidnapper? A train rattles by, trembling the bridge under my feet. I crouch automatically then half-run to the end of the bridge, stooping low behind the wall that separates cars from pedestrians. I turn sharp right down the tree-lined path that runs parallel to the railway line. I walk, taking slow breaths to settle my heart. How does anyone jump from a bridge onto a train? That'd be certain death, surely? They must fake it in the films.

I follow the path curling next to the narrow river. It's getting dark but the sound and smell of the water running next to me is calming. I remember it's called the River Chelt. I learnt that at school when we did our fieldwork project. We all wore wellies and waded in the river catching tiny creatures in nets. Mrs Peters made sure that Raffy and Felix were in separate groups, but it didn't stop them being a pain. I had water tipped in my wellies a couple of times thanks to them, but I didn't care. My feet soon warmed the water up and then it felt comforting. Anyway, I was too absorbed with my magnifying glass inspecting water snails, nymphs, beetles and shrimps.

Back in the classroom Mrs Peters showed us a cool video of freshwater creatures that you can't see unless you've got a powerful microscope. Some of them look a bit like human sperm and eggs. It's mind-boggling to think we all started as tiny as that – one sperm and one egg. Now I'm thinking of my birth mother's letter again and I'm just walking without noticing where I am going, without caring. I sit on a playground swing and push myself high until the chain jolts, then jump off and roll over, pick myself up and run to the playing field exit before a man with a bulging tummy and three dogs gets too close.

I've decided.

I want to skip straight over my birthday and arrive on Monday instead. I want to wake up for school, back to normal, in my own bed. I don't want a fuss. I am going to look for a place to stay out all night. Show them how much I have taken to heart that I am not building my hopes up about the letter. I'm so not fussed about the letter that I'll miss my whole birthday. Maybe I'll look at it another day, maybe I won't.

I need to find a place to hide and sleep. Hide and seek. They'll be looking for me. Or maybe Aunty Bella will stay put in case I come back, not wanting to miss me, not wanting to worry Mum with a phone call. She'll be sipping her mango smoothie and now and again looking up and down the street, leaning over her gate to see if I'm coming. My smoothie will be in the fridge waiting. I can see the orange thick frothiness, smell the fruity perfume. Aunty Bella's whole house has a beautiful, mango glow to it, warm and inviting, smooth and comforting. Then I think of the letter again. It's out of date by ten years. *'She's got her own life now.'*

I force myself to stop this line of thinking. Time to be sensible. I screw my face up trying to work out where to go. Train station – too many cameras. A park – too exposed to dodgy characters and dogs. Shop entrance – ditto. I realise I'm really near my school, which I know inside out.

The carpark is empty. The school is surrounded by a locked green metal fence. I'm sure I can find a way to put one foot in the bolt hole and climb up over it. The daggers on the top edge are still. Inanimate. Not like a snarling dog. I feel an excitement. This could be just an adventure. I'm looking for something to step up on – a recycling caddy will do.

I wonder what it's like staying out all night. On my own. At the back of the school I could get shelter in a doorway and feel safe. Suddenly I start to think about the CCTV cameras and our headteacher, Mrs Banda, calling me in to her office to explain footage of me creeping about on a Saturday night to find shelter.

'Are you having trouble at home, Ches? Have you been turfed out? Did you have an argument? Is there something I can help you with?'

Noooooo. I can't risk school getting involved and Bandage's put-on kind face and soft, purring voice. We all know she is looking out for "bad behaviour" at all times, especially from boys. It's a trap – the soft, cajoling voice before she snaps and bites your head off. She'll call Mum in and the letter will be talked about. It's nobody's business. That letter is written to me. Nobody else. It's all I've got. Get your nosey beaks out.

I march away from the school, relieved not to be climbing that sharp fence. I zigzag down roads, left then right, then left and right again, past endless glowing windows in normal households. Families eating, drinking, watching TV, on the computer, stroking cats on laps, planning their Sunday picnics and visits to sweet, tea-drinking grandparents in the countryside.

There are so many cars parked, dark and empty, in a row next to the kerb. A car makes a good bedroom. I look around and there is no one in the street. My heart is thudding. I quickly try a handle of a car. It's locked. Another. Look. Another. Look. Another. The piercing sound of a car alarm sends me speeding down the street. My legs are scissoring like never before. I feel powerful. An Olympic sprinter.

If I'm caught, I'll be thrown in a police cell. My mum will cry and say, 'Ches, love. What did I do wrong? A car thief. Oh, Ches, my love, look what a mess we're in now.'

I might reply, 'You stole my letter. You stole my privacy.'

THROUGH TOWN

It's OK. Nothing has changed. The distant sound of the car alarm continues then stops. I keep on running, letting my legs decide where we go until I realise, they've brought me to the very Tesco Express that Mum goes to. I dart up a muddy slope and down onto the leafy cycle track towards town. I'm kicking a stone along and wondering if I should just turn around and go home. But Nana Lil is taking up the space and I'm not supposed to be at home.

I kick the stone extra hard and it clangs against a red, metal waste bin on a pole. A woman walking the other way gives me a startled look then shakes her head.

Sorry. I didn't mean to scare you.

I look inside the waste bin. I don't know why. Underneath an empty crisp packet is a black jacket. I pull it out to inspect it. The zip is broken but it's not smelly or dirty. Finding the jacket feels like encouragement so I tie it around my waist and continue to town, past the yellow outdoor gym equipment and through an underpass, spray-painted with bright cartoons. I cross my friend the River Chelt again and find myself in the town centre on a busy summer Saturday night. They are all grownups in sandals, shorts and T-shirts or flowery dresses, smelling of disgusting perfume, laughing, arm in arm, beer cans in hand.

I pass by a man topped with a wild forest of tangled, bushy hair sitting amongst grey, dirty things between a building and railings. A tree is his roof. He's staring at his hands in his lap. He looks like one of those primates you see in the zoo, bored silly, crouched in the corner. Except zoo animals do at least get food shoved in their cage every day.

A mango smoothie pops into my head and I wonder whether this man has ever tasted something so delicious before, and then I remember Aunty Bella. I feel a bit guilty for a moment, but I think about why I am angry. In my head I can hear them telling me, *'Don't build your hopes up, Ches. She's got her own life.'* They know already. Both of them. Maybe even Nana Lil as well. That's why she's up here – to watch the show. They know there's nothing in that letter. Maybe some pathetic "Sorry I never wanted you but have a good life".

Before I can stop it, tears have arrived on my face. I wipe them away with the back of my hand and start jogging so no one can study my face properly. I hear my name and it's a man's voice. I falter, look up and, oh God, it's Raffy's dad, Michael Sideburns. His hugeness is blocking my way. He's wearing a T-shirt with an elephant's head on it, ears covering the shoulders with the trunk all down the middle.

'You all right, mate? Where you off to this time in the evening all by yourself?'

'I'm OK.'

'You don't look OK, Ches. Does your mum know where you are?'

For some reason I can feel tears threatening again, so I dodge and run my fastest down the street, avoiding couples strolling along. I glance over my shoulder, and he's chasing me. This elephant is after me.

'Ches, Ches. Stop.'

But I am fast. That's my super-skill. And I am small. I turn down an alley, squeeze past a big green wheelie bin and duck down, pushing my back against the wall. My heart is galloping, blood whooshing around. I sit still, waiting. I recognise the smell of public toilet stale pee. A huge dark rat, nose to the ground, keeping tight against the opposite wall, runs along nearer to me. It hesitates, nose in the air, smelling the bin, the pee and me, then hurries off down the alley. My heart is steadier now.

There's an outside light high up on the wall and I watch a host of different-sized moths fluttering around it. They can't get enough of the light. Is it the warmth? Are they mistaking it for the moon? Nocturnal moths go nuts for light. There are hundreds. I start to count them but someone's coming. I can smell cigarette smoke. Two older girls are talking to each other.

'It's like, he said Tuesday's no good for me and I said but I can only do Tuesdays late. I have to look after me nan and I'm already doing Fridays and Saturdays. What does he think I am?'

'I'd stick it out if I was you. He can't make you. Family's important, innit? What's he gonna do? Sack you coz he's changed his mind now? Mean git.'

'Hey, there's a kid here. What you doing down here?'

'He's well little, in't he? Nice trainers. You run away? You should go back home, littl'un. Got a home, eh?'

'Sure he has. Look at him. He's clean. Kinda cute with that blond hair and dark skin – nice look. Is that natural or have you bleached it?'

I can't be bothered to answer. I always get asked that stupid question.

'We don't bite. How old are you? Eight, nine?'

'Ten, tomorrow,' I say, and I'm off again, barging past the wheelie bin and the big girls in black T-shirts and small skirts.

Men who smell of man perfume, with large biceps bulging out of clean shirts, spill out of pubs onto the pavement.

I begin to walk along the street as though I know where I'm going, trying not to bring attention to myself. I pretend I've just been asked to go and buy some milk and it's perfectly normal for me to be out walking on my own. Inside I have a gaping hole of sadness and self-pity as I see that everyone else out and about is going to do something for real, with real families. Children are safely at home with a babysitter. No one's pretending to go and buy milk. No one's run away because it's the night before the first time they are going to actually get something from their birth mum. And it's not even worth bothering with. It's probably only a sentence scrawled on a small bit of found paper before running away from me as fast as she could, not even looking back.

I've arrived in ultra-posh Cheltenham. The gigantic houses look like iced wedding cakes and have black metal railing gates stopping people walking onto the sweeping driveways without permission. Each house stands on its own land and has a garage and matching front door with a brand-new swanky car, posed at an angle on the gravel. Like on the adverts. Swanky is one of Mum's words. There are loads of trees everywhere. There's space for trees. And tennis courts and a lake in a big park. I carry on down the road because the road feels safer than a park and I don't reckon Aunty Bella will guess I'm out this way.

Now the houses are new brick and have wooden fences and gates. Still with garages and each on their own piece of land. Not quite so swanky. Children in these houses are cleaning their teeth, kicking off slippers and watching a film, sat up in bed. What am I doing? I should be smashing Aunty Bella at mini table tennis or sat next to her on the sofa watching something on TV. The night before my birthday. I can't just carry on walking out of town.

I take a right off the main road into a street with more houses, and lampposts illuminating the way. A young couple are approaching, talking earnestly, holding hands, passing me without a glance. Way in front of me a teenager is trotting with a black-and-white sheepdog, both keen to get home. I hang back. He turns off and disappears down a front garden path, so I hurry to catch a view of him as he finds his key. But the warm house swallows him and his dog before I can get a good look.

I sit on the low wall, hidden from the house of the dog and boy by a scented, white flower bush. In case anyone sees me in the street I pretend I am waiting for my father to find his keys before we take the dog for a walk. Through the bush I see a tall, slender woman in the front room of the warm house, phone in hand, shutting the blinds. She's shaking her head and frowning, then she's gone. A car is heading down the road towards me and with a shock I recognise the yellow, white and blue of a police car and it's slowing to park on the other side of the road. I leap over the wall and scurry to the side of the house, pushing open a gate, ducking below a lit window, to the densely planted back garden.

What if that's for me? How did they find me? Maybe I got caught on camera when I was trying the cars.

The house is dark at the back, apart from one window upstairs. Perhaps it's the boy's room. I keep my eye on it as I scuttle, bush to bush, towards a garden shed. I hear a dog barking. A strong smell of blackcurrant hits my nostrils as I accidentally snap a couple of branches. I keep still, listening. I continue scrambling low through the garden along with all the other night-time creatures in all the other back gardens looking for food or shelter. I think of badgers and hedgehogs, cats and foxes, all keeping out of the way of humans.

I've accidentally stumbled upon accommodation waiting for me nestled there in a corner. A garden shed is even better than a car. But it's locked. I stare at the padlock feeling foolish; however, something gets me to waggle it anyway. It's unlocked. It looked locked. *Don't ever give up.* Nana Lil always says that whenever anyone is struggling with opening a jar or undoing knots in shoelaces, but then Aunty Bella mutters under her breath that some things it'd be better if Nana Lil did give up. And I think about how she gave up photography. Maybe that's why Nana Lil says it because really, she means don't make the same mistakes I made.

I keep thinking a police officer will flash a torch through the window, but only the bright moon shines in and I can see there is very little space for me to lie down.

I wait, crouching on the floor, ready to pounce up and run, until I feel certain no one is coming, and I need to stretch. Careful not to make too much noise, I ram the three bikes closer to the wall as best I can. I shift dry, dusty boxes, held together by peeling tape, onto the bike saddles. I untie the waste bin jacket from around my middle and put it on.

It's a bit tight under the arms, so I wriggle it off again and lay it on the floor as a thin mattress. Then I delve into a bike bag and extract a flimsy, luminous cycling vest and a dark, plastic cape. I fashion a pillow out of netting sacks flecked with shreds of brittle onion skins and push it into the vest, unrolling the cape to serve as an under-sheet and folding it over my body to make a cover. It's a very presentable job, considering. I don't mind a hard floor at all, and I like the smell of compost and bicycle oil. It smells friendly and like an ordinary family. I wonder what the boy and his family are like but guess I'll never find out, as I'll be off in the early morning well before these Sunday risers are aware that they've even had a night-time visitor.

NIGHT OUT

A church clock strikes eleven. I begin to worry about Aunty Bella waiting for me to come back, and all the time she doesn't know I am safe in a bike shed. I wish I could fly a message through to her brain to stop her phoning Mum, who will freak out, but I can't because my poxy, hand-me-down phone is in my overnight bag with my pyjamas.

I want a pee, so I struggle out of what now feels like nothing more than a big plastic bag, stand up and bang my head on something sharp – really sharp. I'm jumping about, silently screaming whilst holding my head and I crash over onto the bicycles, shifting boxes that clatter alarmingly. I freeze. Surely someone will have heard that racket? Should I run now?

I decide to wait, half-hoping I will be discovered and can spend the night with this family. I'm sure they are nice and understanding. They've got bikes, a boy and a dog. I picture sitting around their kitchen table drinking a smoothie, telling them about how I've got to stay out of the way for one day, it's very important and private, and then I'll go back. I get down to pat the dog, who laps up the attention and rolls over for a tummy rub, legs splayed out, all relaxed.

Somehow because they are really kind and accepting and I don't know them, I end up telling all about the letter and my mother, who I know nothing about except that she left me ten years ago tomorrow. There's a gasp and I look up to see the man and woman looking very strangely at each other and me.

'We think we might know who your mother is.'

I'm enjoying this fantasy very much, but I need to pee. I open the shed door a small amount and look out at the dark shapes in the moonlit garden. There's a faint blue glow from the opened top window. I stare at it for a minute then tiptoe outside and water a leafy bush with a long, long pee, all the time watching the window. A large whirring moth flies by my face very close, making me start. I thoroughly brush my face and hair off, careful around the swelling. My fingers feel the stickiness of blood, which I put to my nose to smell. I'm bleeding, cold, no bed, no bathroom, nobody to help me. I think of the homeless man in the shop entrance doing this every night. All through the year. For years.

I open up the bicycle cape and climb inside with my feet down towards the hood, then wrap the excess around me. I can only lie on my back or one side now, and I have less space because the bikes have slipped. But I am determined to get back to my fantasy and sleep.

A furious barking wakes me. It's so light and the shed looks small and is full of cobwebs and gaps in the walls, letting early-morning sunshine in. I suddenly get that the dog is barking at me, the other side of the door. I'm going to be found because there's no way I'm opening the door. I shove the cape into the bike bag and kick the makeshift pillow under the bikes, stand up and wait.

'Lupin. What are you after, Lupin? Come here.'

I know that voice. He opens the shed door and Raffy is standing there, his hand on the dog's collar.

RAFFY'S PLAN

'Ches, what the hell are you doing here? Lupin, down, sit, sit. Good boy. The police have been out looking for you. You're in deep, deep doo-doo. Did you stay in here all night?'

I'm nodding and I can see a gleam of respect in his eyes.

'Holy mac. What you going to do?'

'I don't know.'

I can't think clearly about why I did this now. I'm feeling excited about Raffy and me talking like this.

'It's my birthday. Today.'

'No way.'

'I wanted to avoid my birthday. I don't like birthdays. Cake and stuff.'

'You just haven't done the right kind of birthday. Birthdays are when you get to do what you really want to do. Look, wait here a minute. Don't go anywhere. I won't tell. Trust me. I'll be back. OK? Come on, Lupin. Come on, boy.'

I nod. He's gone. This is a very strange birthday. My hair is caked with dried blood and the lump has gone down a bit, but it is tender when I press it. I look at my legs and notice some small, oily marks and skin scrapes from my fight with the bicycles last night, and there's a long black streak on my shorts from the dirty chain. Mum's not going to be pleased. In a sort of way, the mess on my clothes is Raffy's doing again – his bike – but this time it's not his fault. I think he might be helping me. I'm feeling nervous and excited, which is a whole lot different to how I normally feel when I start my birthday off.

Soon enough the door opens again. Raffy hands over a plastic bag through the door gap and Lupin pokes his muzzle towards me for a stroke. His eyes are melty brown.

'Eat up. We've got a big day ahead of us. I'm going to help you celebrate your birthday like never before, but you've got to trust me, OK? No cake or any birthday rubbish. Just you and me having fun. Dad's taking Inga to an athletics event in the car and Mum's not the biking and gardening type, so you'll be OK. You can ride a bike, yeh? See if you can lower my saddle. But keep quiet. Tools are in Dad's pannier. Mine's the blue one. I'll ride Inga's. OK?'

'Yeh. OK.'

'See how I'm starting to like you? Not making you ride the girly one?'

'Thanks, Raffy.'

'Be back soon, comrade. Stay low.'

I sit down and open the bag to reveal a croissant and a massive banana but no drink and I'm so thirsty. I spy a metal bottle on Raffy's bike, wheedle it out of the holder and guzzle the stale water within. After breakfast, I begin the task of lowering his bike saddle. It's like one of those plastic cracker games where you move one square only to find you have to move another load of squares to get the first square properly out of the way.

All done whilst limiting the noise. In spite of interlocking pedal messes, I manage to get the other side of Inga's bike in order to put in the effort I need to shift Raffy's bike saddle lever. But it won't budge. Nana Lil pops into my head with her "don't give up" mantra. My hand gets red and indented from the effort, so I wrap a cloth around it and try again.

Raffy's going to think I'm a weakling if I can't even do this, but it's impossible. Why am I so small and weak? Who do I take after? I wish I had a photograph of my parents, then I could see where my brown skin and skinny legs and arms all come from. Are they both brown like me, or is one of them black and one white? Why have I got tight curls that are blond? I found out on the internet that there are loads of dark-skinned people, much darker than me, with blond curly hair in the Pacific Islands off Australia – but that's the other side of the world. There's no one in Cheltenham that looks like me.

Lupin's barking, but it isn't at me. What if Raffy's lied to me, and he's called the police and now they've come for me? It looks like I'm trying to steal a bike. First cars and now a bike. How am I going to explain all this? Oh God, sorry, Mum, sorry, so sorry. Social services will get involved and I'll end up in a children's home and then on the street. My heart is thundering, and I feel sick. Doors slam and a car leaves.

Raffy opens the shed door, squeezes in then shuts the door.

'Hey, what's up with you? You OK, Mr Trunk? Relax. I told you I'd be back. You can trust me. We're almost like cousins, you and me. Not blood, but you know, kind of in a weird, could-have-been, mixed-up kind of way. Well, maybe just the surname, but good enough, eh? Cousins. All right?'

I nod and swallow. I'm sure we are nowhere near cousins looking at us, but I remember that comforting fantasy I had last night where I made Raffy's mum my aunty, though I had no idea it was his mum at the time. So maybe in a strange, other-worldly way we are cousins – Ches and Raffy Trunk. That'd make it my dad where I got the tight curls and brown skin from.

'Look, mate, you'll have to have Inga's bike coz there's no crossbar on a girl's bike. I realise you're too short for mine.'

Whilst Raffy deals with the saddle lever on Inga's bike I watch his muscles flex and think that he wouldn't even have existed if his dad, Michael, and my mum had stayed together. Michael would have been my adopted dad. All those coincidences and chances and decisions and actions make a human being happen and it could so easily be a different outcome with a tiny change of circumstances. What is my how-I-happened story? No one to ask. One of the lost stories.

'Right, that should do. Now, listen, this is the plan. I'm meant to be with Felix today coz Mum wants some chilling time on her own. So, I rung him and told him it's not happening, but I told Mum I'm cycling over there. With me so far? But you are a wanted man. The police are looking for you so, Ches, trust me, it's for your own good – you need to put this stuff on.'

He pulls out his mum's fancy-dress wig. It's very long and shiny, synthetic black with a blunt fringe. Then he reveals a girl's blue-and-white stretchy T-shirt dress.

'I can't wear that. I'll look an idiot.'

But somehow, I'm letting Raffy pull the dress down over my shorts whilst I gently adjust the long black wig over my sore lump. Raffy's eyes are gleaming as he tweaks my new fringe. He seems proud of his crazy disguise.

'That is an ace look, Ches. What's your name for today then? What do you fancy? Cherie? Lavinia? You choose.'

'Sara.'

'OK. Sara it is. Sara, my cousin, who is having chemo and has to wear a wig coz there is no way that hair looks real. Happy?'

'Happy.'

GETTING READY

I'm waiting for Raffy to come and take my bike down the street for me, then occupy his mum whilst I walk through their garden and wait by the bike for him. He's really thought it through and I'm feeling confident I can leave the shed behind, safe in Raffy's company for the day. A woman is whistling and coming closer. Please don't come in the shed. Please don't come in the shed. Not now.

'Do you want a hand, Mum? With the washing?'

'That'd be nice. What are you after then? Very suspicious behaviour, Raffy, helping your mother without being asked.'

'Nothing. Just feel like helping.'

'Mmm. A likely story.'

Raffy's mum starts whistling again. She's good. I recognise the tune from the radio.

'Well, there is one thing. You know me and Felix are hanging out today? Can I have a sleepover?'

'It's a school night, Raffy. School tomorrow and I've got a full-on workday on Monday. I can't be kept up with you two cavorting about all night.'

'I don't mean a sleepover here. I meant at Felix's. Give you a nice quiet evening without me. And Felix's parents are strict about not messing about. Please, Mum. Felix asked me. We can do our homework together.'

'You told your dad you'd done your homework.'

'I have, except we've got to prepare for a test, so I'd like to be able to test each other. It's not the same as trying to learn it on your own. Felix's parents are happy about me staying.'

'I'll have to ring them to say thank you and make sure it is OK. It's very nice of them.'

'Please don't hassle them, Mum. Dad's already talked to his mum about today at least twice. You know where I'll be. They wouldn't have said yes if they weren't happy about it.'

'OK. But you can take one of your dad's loaves as a small present. He won't mind.'

'Nice one. Thanks, Mum. Why don't you go in, have your shower, sit down and enjoy a coffee, and I'll finish the washing? Go on, Mum. I can do it.'

'Good grief, Raffy. Are you sure you're all right? Not got mixed up with Inga?'

'I'm just happy.'

'Well, good for you. Enjoy it whilst you can.'

I feel a bit jealous about the sleepover. Through a slit in the shed wall I watch Raffy peg a set of scarlet towels onto the rotary washing line and walk away without a second look towards me.

Minutes later he's back to collect Inga's bike and two water bottles to fill.

'I've got to be quick with this bike while she's in the bathroom. Count to one hundred – no, make it two hundred – and then turn right down the street and wait by Inga's bike.

You can push it slowly along. I'll be as quick as I can. Don't give up on me. Wait. Understood?'

'Yes. Understood.'

I forget to start counting straight away so have to guess where to start from. I'm bursting for a pee. One hundred and ninety-nine, two hundred. I open the door and quickly head for the hedge, where I shuffle my dress up and release a torrent of steamy, frothy pee. It's going on for ages, drowning some pansies, and I didn't allow for this time in my counting. Come on, come on. Finally, I pull my dress down and scoot towards the front garden, up the path and turn right without a backward glance. My thick, black, ridiculously long hair is whooshing behind me. I run to the bike, grab hold of the handlebars and start pushing it away from the house.

I am Sara. I've got to wear this wig because I have cancer. I know I'm very young. My parents are finding it very hard, but I am being brave. My cousin and I are having a day out together on our bikes. It might be the last time we can do it. It's fifty-fifty whether I live or not, but no one likes to talk about that. We're just trying to be positive.

Then I see Raffy cycling towards me along the pavement. He shouts:

'On your bike, Sara. Follow me.'

BIKE RIDE

I wouldn't admit it to most people, but there's something really good about riding a girl's bike that is easy to mount and dismount, whilst wearing a stretchy, striped dress and long hair flying out in the wind. I am no longer Ches. I am Sara. It's not like I want to be a girl or anything, but it's making me think about the stupid, strict rules we have to follow to prove we're a boy. Why are girls allowed to wear jeans and T-shirts and boys can't wear dresses and have long plaits? Most boys go through their whole lives not experiencing this, and I reckon they're missing out.

I feel a gleeful buzzing in my body as my knees pound round and round, taking me speedily along. The road is lined both sides by pavements and neatly clipped hedges ballooning above short walls. I don't have to think about which way to go as I pursue the yellow T-shirt on the bike ahead. I'm really loving my birthday.

We weave in and out of a row of eight gigantic stone pillars in front of a fancy old building used for weddings, then shoot off onto the bicycle track I've been down hundreds of times before. I avoid pushchairs, and little kids on scooters or trainer bikes out for a trundle next to the lakes. Raffy cycles off the tarmac and onto the dry mud path next to the railings and I copy him weaving between any trees we can.

I want to know where we are going. We're following the River Chelt the other side of the railings. This track ends up next to my mum's Tesco. Is Raffy tricking me and really, he's taking me home? I didn't know he even knew where I lived. What's he up to? I speed up and curve around to a stop in front of his bike, making him brake hard.

'What are you doing? Where are you taking me?'

'What are *you* doing, you nutter? You nearly had me off.'

Raffy gets his balance then pulls my head towards him and hisses into my wig hair, 'Stop making a fuss. You'll blow your cover. Now trust me. We're going on an adventure. A birthday adventure.'

'This comes out really close to my home.'

'So? Have you seen yourself in the mirror? Obviously not. No one's going to recognise you, for sure.'

He lets go of me and smiles as he pushes my fringe from my eyes. I have a weird moment of seeing him as the father he might one day be.

'Come on. Come on, Sara. Follow me. Nearly there. It's OK. You can trust me.'

I toss his hand away with a flick of my head. 'Really? And why should I? You've never been nice to me before.'

'Never realised you were worth it.'

Standing and straddling Inga's bike, I can't work out how I'm supposed to feel right now. Do I just drop the bike, pull the wig off and run back home? Face all that letter and worry stuff? Deep inside I can feel a hard, little lump of badness.

Raffy begins to hum a tune. Within three notes I've got it. I sigh to hide my grin, jump on my bike and join in singing.

'Happy birthday to me.'

My eyes are scooting about all over the place checking for anyone who might recognise me as we head up off the cycle track and cross the road away from Tesco. Raffy comes to a halt in front of Cheltenham Spa railway station and tells me to hang on to his bike for five minutes. He's going for a pee, he says. I can't see anyone around who I know so I take the opportunity to have a quick look at what he has in his panniers. One has food and the other pannier has clothes rammed in? Hard to tell without getting it all out. Raffy returns.

'I've bought you a birthday present. Just now. Come on. We're catching the next train to a secret, special birthday destination.'

'But Raffy, I don't think we should leave Cheltenham.' I sound whiny even to myself.

'Hey, Sara. We're cousins, right? And I'm going to look after you. I've done this plenty of times with my dad. I know what I'm doing. You do trust me, don't you?'

I look at him standing there and he looks forlorn. I want to see his cheery face. I want to share my birthday with him.

'Can't we do something around here? We could cycle to Cleeve Hill. It's brilliant.'

'No, we can't. I'm not taking you to do something you've done a thousand times before. On your birthday you have to do something different and exciting, preferably with an element of surprise and organisation from someone else who cares about you having fun. I've spent a load of my own money on the tickets. Are you telling me you want to waste my money?'

'No. Sorry. I just got scared for a moment.'

I don't tell him that I'm still scared. I don't say, '*Why are you doing this for me? You didn't care about me when you put a dead slow-worm in my PE bag.*'

'No worries, Sara. You're a girl and sometimes girls get scared, but it's OK. I know what I'm doing. You said you didn't want birthday cake and all that fuss. I'm doing my best to give you a fun birthday time to remember.'

That is weird hearing that "girls get scared" business. I look over my shoulders to see who might have heard, but there's only an Asian family busy trying to collapse a pushchair and a man with a Zimmer frame making his way into the station.

I whisper, 'You know I'm still a boy, Raffy.'

'I know – you were only pretending to be scared. Now let's get onto the platform. We've got fifteen minutes to wait for the train.'

I need a bit of time to think on my own about all this, so I lean my bike against the platform wall next to the big round "Help Point" and tell Raffy I'm off to the loo as I head towards the men's.

'Sara, the girls' toilets are that way, OK? Don't be long. I'll be waiting for you.'

'Holy macaroni', as my friend George would say. I look back at Raffy and he waves me forwards with a big grin on his face. I get to the door with the symbol of a stick woman on it and hesitate, look back again, and Raffy has his phone out and is taking my photo. I dive into the toilets, see a woman glance at me as she adjusts her blouse in the mirror, take a quick turn and lock myself in a cubicle.

I hitch my dress up, drop my shorts, sit down on the toilet, girl-style, and poke my willy down to pee. It all feels a bit unreal. It's only just over twelve hours since I left Aunty Bella's, but now, I'm a year older, turned into a girl having chemo, seem to be the best friend of my sworn enemy and am heading on a magical mystery tour. I grin to myself and ignore the niggling doubts squirming around my guts as I flush the loo and pull my dress down straight, before opening the cubicle door.

TRAIN JOURNEY

I'm sitting next to the window, looking at the landscape whizzing away from me as though I'm falling down Alice's rabbit hole.

I glance at the words scrolling along above the door – "Calling at Gloucester, Cam and Dursley, Yate, Bristol Parkway, Filton Abbey Wood, Bristol Temple Meads" – and I think of Mum, Nana Lil and Aunty Bella spending my birthday without me. It feels like the further we travel away from them the smaller they get, and I worry they will disappear altogether. They'll just become a thin memory and then nothing. I wonder if that's what I've become for my birth mother – nothing? Hang on, she didn't even get to know me. I didn't *become* nothing. I was always nothing.

'Where're we getting off Raffy? Gloucester?'

He does his nervous cough, puts his fingers to his lips, leans forward and whispers, 'Gloucester's boring. Do you like the seaside, Sara? Me and Dad love going to the seaside. This is what we do. Take our bikes on the train, cycle to the seaside and have a nice time, just him and me, father and son, enjoying some bonding time. That's what we're going to do.'

A woman is spooning some pale-pink goo from a little pot into her toddler's mouth, who is busily turning a horribly loud and irritating electronic plastic toy on and off, on and off. No one else has chosen to sit anywhere near this noise, but I'm watching them in the next seating compartment and wondering if this little boy has a father? And does he see him?

It's like Raffy can read my mind.

'Do you miss not having a dad? To do boy stuff with?'

'Not really. You don't miss what you haven't ever had.'

'So, when you see all the other dads you don't think, *I wish I had a dad like everyone else?*'

'Not everyone has got a dad, have they? And some people wish they didn't have the dad they've got. I wouldn't want a cruel dad or a drunk dad. I've got a really good mum, so I think I'm lucky. She's brilliant.'

Raffy looks at me, thinking about this. 'But she couldn't have babies, could she? That's not that great. Not for her.'

'She had me, though. She did become a mum, coz she had me, see?'

'Yeh, I see. But that's not the same, is it? She wanted to have a real son or daughter. Dad said she tried loads, but they all died. Even before they were born… I wonder who your real dad was? Probably *was* a drunk or cruel and your real mum left him. And then she didn't want to be reminded of him by having you around. Maybe that's what happened.'

I watch how if you look far away everything moves slowly but if you focus near the train, the hedgerow goes very fast. I flick my eyes up and down several times, changing my viewpoint, until I feel a wave of tiredness. The train is soothing and very warm.

'Wakey, wakey, Sara. Time to get our bikes.'

I blindly follow Raffy's yellow-covered back and struggle to angle my bike towards the door and get off the train. I follow him through the crowd to the station lift and we wait.

'Platform 4 – then before you know it, cycling to the seaside. Sara, what ice-cream do you like?'

'Mint choc chip.'

'Me too.' He smiles at me and adjusts my wig a little.

Sitting on the second train I feel like we've come too far now to turn back. I'm in Raffy's hands.

'Calling at Nailsea and Backwell, Yatton, Worle, Weston-Super-Mare…'

'Tickets, please? All passengers from Bristol Temple Meads. Thank you. Thank you. You kids on your own?'

'My dad's waiting for us at Weston. He biked there, but it's too far for my cousin. She's not very strong, are you, Sara?'

I shake my head and look down at my lap. Raffy coughs every couple of seconds. I sense the inspector looking at me and I almost want him to rip my wig off and say, 'You're that missing boy the police are looking for, aren't you?'

'OK. Tickets, please.'

He's gone, and with him what feels like my very last chance to stop all this.

We push our bikes to the front of Weston-Super-Mare station, and all of a sudden, I feel like I'm on holiday. A cycle track sign is pointing us to the beach. No matter what, I always feel a flutter of excitement when I first smell the sea – and then I see it.

I can't believe we're at the seaside.

CYCLE TRACK 33

Wiggling to avoid Sunday dawdlers, we are cycling along the seafront promenade past stalls overflowing with bright plastic beach toys. Raffy seems to know where he's going, and I do my best to keep up with his yellow T-shirt as I don't know what I'd do if I lost him. We head for the cycle track and I feel a lot better now the sea breeze is blowing in my face and my legs are pedalling hard. I can almost ignore the heavy feeling in my heart. I nearly collide into the back of Raffy as he brakes to a stop outside a café.

'Choc mint ice-cream? Better than birthday cake any day.'

I'm licking the minty cold sweetness, crunching on chocolate flecks and reading about Cycle Track 33 on a wall poster. It was opened less than a year ago.

'How often have you done this ride with your dad?'

'Loads.'

'Loads? What, more than ten?'

I don't know why I'm trying to catch him out. What am I going to do even if he's lying?

'About that. I know what I'm doing. Any wally could do it. Follow the blue cycle signs. Look, let's have our picnic lunch soon. I'm still hungry.'

He wipes his mouth with his arm and jumps on his bike before I've even finished. I have to cycle like a nut to catch up. I struggle getting through ridiculously tricky gates on my own and at one point I'm in a hot sweat pushing my bike forwards into a sharply angled gap, pulling the gate past the end of my bike and then trying to back it up one-handed. As I grab my bike to stop it falling, I get long strands of hair caught in my fingers and the wig is pulled off, exposing my real hair. The long black hair gets caught up in the wheel spokes as I try to steer backwards. It looks like some terrifying bike-eating spider thing. A man in orange and black Lycra running shorts holds the gate for me and with difficulty I pick the back of the bike up to stop the wig getting any more tangled up.

'You all right, kiddo? You've got a right mess there. Let me help you.'

'No, I'm OK. Thanks.'

'Come on. Turn this thing over so we can get at it. Who are you with, then? Anyone?'

'Yes. My cousin. He's ahead. I'm catching him up.'

My face is burning with shame at being caught out with a girl's wig on and a dress, but at the same time I'm enjoying air to my head. That wig is so hot. Good to have a break from it.

'This is an impossible mess. I'm going to have to rip it. Give it a good old pull. Will you be in trouble if it doesn't come out perfect?'

'I don't know. It's not mine. It's my cousin's mum's.'

'Hmm. I'm Mark, by the way. And you?'

'Ches.'

'Ches. Fabulous name for a girl, that. Here goes. Hold on to the bike as best you can.'

The wig comes free and I ram it on my head as the man upturns Inga's bike.

'Thanks,' I call whilst scooting away from further questions, past a family cycling towards me. I look over my shoulder and I can see Mark leaning on the gate and watching me, his hand shading his eyes. He gives me a thumbs-up. I cycle as fast as I can. He thought I was a girl even without my wig on. It's the purple bike and the dress. I look like a girl. I'm not sure what I think about this information.

Raffy is sitting on the grass, his bike flung down to the side, and he is tearing into a loaf of brown bread.

'What kept you?' He grins.

'Nothing. Just taking it easy.'

We eat chunks of solid home-made bread smeared with peanut butter, washed down with water.

'Good, eh? My dad says he did this all the time when he was a boy. Just go off for the whole day with a packed lunch. His parents never knew where he was. Who he was with. He said it was the making of him. He says we're too cosseted. These days.'

'Cosseted?'

'Yeh. Driven everywhere. No adventure. No fending for ourselves. He says everyone's too scared from all the bad news and it makes us prisoners in our own lives. We're not prisoners now, are we, Sara?'

'Can you stop calling me Sara when we're on our own? There's no need, is there? Call me Ches.'

'OK, Sara.'

'Ches. Or I'll call you Veronica.'

Raffy laughs and I laugh too.

'Let's get going. I want to show you the biggest beach ever. Come on… "Ches".'

We cycle over a bridge crossing a river and along the track, past a field with rows and rows of white caravans and mobile homes sitting side by side. We cycle on and on down country lanes and across a road, all the time following the cycle signs of Route 33. I'm beginning to get weary of this when we finally arrive at a sandy pathway where we have to get off and push. My arms begin to ache. Then the sparkling sea, the vast sandy beach and white gulls circling the blue sky take my breath away, and I forget any tiredness and any doubts.

'This is the making of us, Ches. We did this on our own.'

'Yeh. We did.'

CHIPS

The cold, June sea stings and prickles my skin. I am up to my knees in a sparkling wash of sandy-coloured water, clutching on to my dress and looking out at the vast seascape. I fantasise that the water is completely transparent and whatever is down there is visible, like when you walk past gigantic tanks in an aquarium. I pretend I can see jellyfish and crabs, shoals of silver fish and larger predatory sharks. I imagine broken ribs of sunken boats decorated with lime-green seaweed ribbons and blue or orange plastic fishing debris jutting out of the sand. A mermaid with brown sandy skin and long curly hair, fairish like mine, is swimming towards me. She's holding a shell out for me to take and although I know this is all in my head my knees begin to shake, and tears spring out of nowhere. She has legs imprisoned in a fish tail. It's impossible for her to join my world.

I slowly twig that Raffy is calling me by my girl name, so I scoop water up and splash my face, wetting a good deal of my black wig hair in the process. Then I skip-run, whooshing through the shallow sea, back to where our bikes are propped up against a pole.

'See that land jutting out into the sea? Right the very end is where we're going. Brean Down. There's a cycle track the other side, all the way along. Let's go.'

I nod and do a making-my-lips-disappear kind of smile.

'We might catch the café open for some chips, if we hurry.'

Cars with doors gaping wide open are dotted at odd angles across the hard sand. We cycle past clusters of people on beach towels, candy-striped wind barriers, plastic cool boxes and sun umbrellas planted next to each car. I can see my mum shaking her head at the "craziness and laziness of humans" and I wish she could see me speeding across the beach. I wish Aunty Bella and Nana Lil were waiting with her at the café, with plates of fish and chips, ready for us all to tell them the story of our adventure. I'd let them sing happy birthday. Raffy and I'd cycle along the Down path whilst they walked on the beach and then we'd put the bikes on the back of Mum's car and drive home. Maybe I'd invite Raffy to my flat for a sleepover in the lounge.

As we sit outside and share a plate of chips, a crowd of captive, exotic birds fills the air with whistles and chatter from a nearby aviary. There's a scattering of bungalows, two cafés and a toilet block, but we can't find where the birdsong is coming from.

'Could be fake. A sound installation,' says Raffy.

'Why would they do that?'

'Why not? It's weirder keeping real birds locked up.'

'S'pose.'

'Imagine not being able to fly. Someone's clipped your wings or given you a mean, small cage.'

'And you can see the sparrows flying around and the gulls. From your cage. That's bad.'

'I want to fly.'

'Sometimes I have a bit of a feeling that I can. If I try hard enough and tip forward maybe I can.'

Raffy looks at me for a time and I think I might have revealed something that makes me seem crazy.

'I know I can't fly really. It's only a kind of dream or a fantasy. It'd be brilliant to be able to fly, wouldn't it?'

'Maybe we can. Come on, let's cycle to the end of the headland. I want to show you something.'

We leave the empty chip plate, shiny with grease, and grab our bikes. I glance back at the table and can almost imagine Nana Lil sneaking a glug of alcohol into her coffee from a bottle she keeps in her handbag. Mum and Aunty Bella are waving at me and Mum is blowing kisses. But there's only a sparrow there, picking crumbs from my plate. We cycle past a hastily scrawled sign tacked to a fence telling us the "bird park" is closed for refurbishment.

My legs have gone a bit weak. It is hard work pushing my bicycle pedals over the big stones and dips in the track. I must keep up with Raffy.

THE FORT

There are black cows, heads bowed deep in the green grass, silhouetted against sparkling blue-grey sea as we plough our way along a rough stony track. It's a long, bumpy, arduous ride, and although I know from the beach view earlier that we are cycling down a narrow strip of land jutting into the sea, it doesn't seem like that now. There's a steep hill immediately to our left hiding the beach we were on. If I look out to the right, in the distance I can see the pier at Weston-Super-Mare and beyond that, miles away, is Mum, Aunty Bella, Nana Lil and the letter.

What's in the letter?

Aunty Bella likes to use the "worst-case scenario/best-case scenario" strategy for when she is tackling something or trying to help Mum stop worrying. When I think about possible bad things my birth mother might have written my brain gets tangled up. It's not like clear story threads appear. It's more of a horrible spaghetti mess. It always leads me to worrying about ending up as a sad, homeless person sitting alone in a doorway, never having enough to eat.

I watch some seagulls wheeling around in the sky for a minute then start to think of best-case scenarios. This is what Aunty Bella and Mum were steering me away from. I know, by what they've hinted at, that the letter won't produce a happy story, but what would my happy story be anyway? What could possibly be a good ending to my birth mother leaving me on day one of my life? I stand up off the saddle, start to push my legs hard and speed up my bike to overtake Raffy, who is ambling along on his fat tyres and whistling.

A number of flat concrete slabs like giant, unmarked graves are laid out next to each other down on the right, facing the bay. Foundations of buildings left behind after the wind has blown away the walls and roofs. Or maybe there were only ever the floors. Then in front of me I see a couple of low, stone buildings with a dozen or more empty windows in a row, stretching across the headland. The smaller one on the right has a flat roof and blocked-in windows, but the wider one is open to the air. It looks unfinished. But maybe it's a ruin.

Raffy pulls up to a stop next to me. 'This is the fort. Brean Down Fort. Do you like it?'

'Cool. Can we go in?'

Without a word Raffy starts pedalling towards what looks like a drawbridge slicing between the buildings. I follow, eager to keep up with him. Raffy locks my bike to his against a wall. The dark stone looks like hardened slabs of bruised meat piled up.

'This is an old war station. Can you imagine firing guns at invading ships? Pow, pow, bumph! End of.'

He runs through a courtyard and up a grassy bank whilst I stop by an information display to find out the history of this place. I have imagined death and destruction, amputees, prisoners of war and head bandages. I can almost smell blood. But I find out that no ships were ever gunned down from here. The French never arrived. Nor was it useful in the Second World War except for practice.

I watch a family with a golden Labrador begin to head back across the walkway between the main buildings and on up the hill. There are a couple of older women with walking poles still here, but I can't see anyone else. Raffy's nowhere in sight, but our bikes are still there leaning against the wall, so I feel safe enough.

I climb the steep, rugged bank and discover strange construction remains. There are big, geometric concrete shapes, oddly angled low walls and bits of chunky metal, fashioned for a long-forgotten purpose. With my back to the fort and facing the glittering seascape I imagine I'm a soldier on watch. I'm looking out for Napoleon's first ironclad ship, rumoured to be on its way from France to blow up our defenceless wooden ships. I populate the sea with huge, three-masted ships, their cream sails billowing like bedsheets on a washing line. Am I bored or am I constantly on high alert because any moment now my sighting of the enemy ship *Gloire* will initiate a war attack? I raise my hands to make a telescope shape and scan the horizon. Nothing.

I lower my telescope to search the low-lying craggy, black rocks where the peninsula meets the water. I am looking for pirates or ship-wrecked sailors dragging themselves out of the sea, but then my heart races because I actually do see someone scrambling around.

It's Raffy and he is dangerously near the waves. My strongest shouting is instantly swallowed by the wind and my frantic arm waving is lost on Raffy, who is focused on climbing across the rocks. I watch, paralysed by the thought of him drowning and the terrible consequences. The two women I saw earlier are marching up the hill behind me, already as small as sheep in the distance.

We are alone.

A few crows are laughing at me from the sky.

INCOMING TIDE

To me it feels like we need to be heading back to Cheltenham. Urgently. We've got a train to catch and many miles of cycling to even reach the station. The tide has travelled a long way up the beach. The early evening sky is a background of pale blue swept with soft pinks and patches of apricot, making the flattened-out black rocks below look even darker.

Raffy's standing space is lessening wave by wave with the incoming tide. He turns to look up at me, and beckons. I stab my wrist numerous times with my finger indicating as clearly as I can that it's time to go. Then I plant my feet firmly apart and put my fists on my waist, elbows sticking out. I draw my lips in tight. This is exactly what my mum does when she looks at the state of my room before blitzing it, or when she discovers ruined games kit courtesy of Raffy. It's so weird to think that he did all that.

It looks like he's laughing at me as he tilts his head back and sways around, arms out, palms up to get me to look at where we are. I lean my head back. The sky is hurling pastel ribbons of light far out across the sea. In town too many buildings hide the sky and the land. Here it feels like I could breathe an enormous lungful of sea air, pitch forward and rise, buoyed up by the wind current. Fly across the sunset-coloured sea, my long, black wig streaming out behind me.

I look down and the rocks are bare. I feel blood drain from my face and my heart pump in my chest. Raffy's gone. The sea crashes and foams across the rocks and I feel sick to the stomach.

Pulling the wig off as I go, I run to where the grass ends, and the craggy edge of the headland tumbles down towards the sea-smoothed rocks below. I keep seeing a giant wave envelop his small body and drag him into the depths of the ocean. I have to turn away from the sea to use both my hands and feet to climb down. I'm shaking and murmuring to myself. 'I'm so sorry, Mum. I didn't know he was going down there. He shouldn't have gone. I'm sorry, Mum. I shouldn't have run away. I'm really, really sorry. Mum. Mum?'

I'm careful and as steady as I can be. I don't want to break my leg or my back and die here on the rocks below, pecked by gulls and crows, nibbled on by crabs. Already, sea creatures will be sniffing around Raffy's rapidly cooling body as the tide draws him in and out. Perhaps his corpse will be flung on to the beach sand, where a jogger will find him. 'I'm so, so sorry. Mum. What shall I do? I've got to do something. What shall I do?'

Landing on the flattened rock I turn around to search the waves, which are only two or three metres in front of me, hoping to catch a glimpse of his yellow T-shirt. I realise there is nothing I can do. Even if I saw him, what would I do? I don't want to die. I bellow at the sea, all the time searching through my tears for a sighting of yellow cloth even far, far out.

'Stupid, stupid Raffy. Why did you do that? You stupid, stupid boy.'

A splash of cold spray reaches my shins and I stumble back a little, still scanning the sea, hoping to glimpse Raffy's body amongst the waves. My mind is conjuring up Raffy's grinning head bobbing up to the surface. I can almost see him waving, beckoning me to join him. 'Come on in, Ches. Don't be a girl. It's fun.' I blink and the gallons and gallons and gallons of water are still there heaving back and forth, but there is no boy. He's gone.

The roaring attack of the incoming tide forces me to turn towards the rocks I must climb. Seagulls are still flying above. I am still on Brean Down. But honestly it doesn't feel like I am really here. Not like I am actually awake and living this horrible scene. My legs are wobbling uncontrollably as though I have no bones, no muscles – just two skinny tubes of blubber leaning against the rockface, beginning to bend under the weight of my body. I imagine I can feel the wet breath of a gigantic sea monster closing in behind me, ready to gobble me up. I'm a tiny insect. I could fall back and let it devour me.

Just when I begin to fold downwards, my body jolts awake as a soft, black crow flies into my face from above. I scream. All of a sudden, I am alert. I recognise the "crow" as the wig I flung off earlier. The wind must have blown it over the edge. I pick it up and momentarily think of Raffy's grinning face as he handed it to me in the shed only this morning. It feels a world away, all that. Now he's dead. Drowned.

I start to scramble up the steep rockface with the wig stuffed in the back of my shorts. I've got to tell someone what's happened. I can see Raffy's dad shouting in my face, trying to shake an explanation out of me, and Mum standing by, head buried in her hands, hot with deep shame.

I struggle to heave myself up, pulling on the grass at the top and pushing up with my feet against craggy rock surface. At last I'm lying flat on my stomach, feeling exhausted and alone. I have a sense of the earth stretching miles and miles down below me and that I could be sucked into it and that that might solve everything. Make everything disappear. But my bony ribs push into the earth with each wretched breath I take. My nose presses hard into the grass.

I become aware of a presence. I look up and see someone a little way away who looks exactly like Raffy Trunk, standing on the grass, legs akimbo, arms folded. He's looking at me with one eyebrow raised. It doesn't make sense. My brain is racing to try to fathom it out.

He coughs.

I'm frowning.

No words arrive. Instead I feel a huge wave of warmth drive up my neck into my face and a forceful pulsing in my ears. I pull myself to standing. He's looking at me and shaking his head.

'You got yourself in a right old state, didn't you? Nice you care. If a bit stupid.'

'How… how… how did you? How did you do it?'

'Hid around the side of the rocks and waited until you'd gone down before I shinnied up. I was surprised it was so easy. You weren't even looking. You were so convinced I'd been swept out to sea. Thought you'd look around and spot me. You'd be a useless soldier.'

'I could have died.'

'You didn't, though, did you? It's only hide and seek, Ches. Lighten up. I even gave you a clue when I flung the wig down at you.'

'I hate you.'

'Yeah, well. Bad loser. Just a game and you lost.'

It's not easy to sort this out in my head. I want to remind him it's meant to be my birthday.

I should've gone to the lido with Aunty Bella, Nana Lil and Mum. Raced Aunty Bella in the cold pool until we both got knackered. We'd sit caped in towels, smelling of chlorine, and play cards, the four of us, like a family. I could have had proper fish and chips. Mum would've tried so hard to be cheery the whole day. She'd be doing her best to keep her mum sober, stop Aunty Bella from throttling Nana Lil and all the time reminding me that I'm... well, that it's my birthday. Can't be any fun for Mum – my glum-faced birthdays.

I look at Raffy and shout at him, 'It wasn't a game to me. I hate you.'

I didn't say, '*I hate myself too. For being such an idiot.*'

THE JOKER

It's hard to forgive. Even if all the nasty little tricks Raffy has ever done to me were swept into one pile it wouldn't be anywhere near as big as what he's just done. I don't want to even look at him now. I wish he were dead. I wish he had drowned.

He's left me for five minutes to "cool down", but too soon I can feel him coming back up behind me. I remain arms folded, still fuming, staring out at the sea.

'You'll see the funny side soon enough. It was just a bit of fun. Don't get all girly on me. You should have seen your face. You really, really thought you'd seen a ghost, didn't you?'

Peals of laughter, but I'm not laughing. I'm angry.

'Look, Sara—'

I swing around to face him and shout, '*Ches!* Don't you know when to stop? My name's Ches. And *you* look. I want to go back now. It's late and we've got to leave – now.'

He's standing there like a big ape grinning. I hate him.

I run off towards the bikes, determined to search in his pannier for some alternative clothing to this ridiculous dress.

I don't want anything to do with him. I wish I'd never come on this trip and I'd gone home instead. Spent my birthday with Mum. Mum. She'll be out of her mind with worry. It's all his stupid, stupid fault.

I put on a black, puffy, sleeveless jacket thing and over my shorts I pull some jogging bottoms that are too big for me. I don't care. I roll them up, stuff the dress into the trousers.

Then I see it.

My front tyre is completely flat.

The ape approaches.

'That's what I was trying to tell you. A puncture. And what's more, I don't have a pump.'

I kick him hard in the shin, but he's quick to grab me and push me down onto the rough concrete ground, banging my shoulder. I grab his face and squeeze with furious force before he pins my arms down and sits heavily on top of me. Both of us are breathing hard and staring at each other. He prepares a gob of spit in his mouth and lets it dribble onto the side of my face while I'm straining to turn away. I feel his weight lighten as he moves his leg over to stand and I scramble up, ready to direct a hard jet of spit into his face. It's a good shot. He wipes his eye then leaps forwards, pushing me against the building. He secures me with his body, and his one hand locks my chin upwards. I squeeze my eyes shut, determined not to scream out, as my bike shed injury is pressed against hard stone.

'Do you know why I hate you, little Trunk?'

I open my eyes.

'Coz I'm adopted?'

Raffy looks at me quizzically for a moment then starts nodding. 'Yeh, I reckon that's it. You're adopted. An unwanted little piece of poo. That's exactly it. And your mum can go and get herself a replacement from the little pieces of poo shop if you don't find your way back from here. Maybe she's doing that right now.'

'My mum did want me. She does want me. I know she does.'

'Really. You think that? Or does she want something else? Something a bit more exciting, perhaps. Remember, your real mum didn't want you, did she? Maybe, just maybe, there's something wrong with you.'

I have a strange sensation that this isn't really happening at all. It's as if I'm watching two small creatures down below, from way up in the sky. I'm an eagle or a red kite and I'm wondering whether it's worth diving down to snatch the fatter one or not bother at all.

Raffy loses interest and releases me, prodding my chest with his stabby finger before strolling away.

I trace my fingers over my bike shed cut and inspect the slight stickiness left on my fingertips. Mum would be sure to clean my wound up if I was home now.

I remember a conversation Mum and I had one night-time after I'd woken from a bad dream and sought out her comforting bed. As she'd cuddled me and I'd felt deliciously secure like a mouse in a nest of cosy, shredded wool, I'd asked in a very small voice, 'Do you regret adopting me?'

She'd pulled me closer and spoken into my mousy ear. 'It takes a few minutes to make a baby if you're fertile. You don't even have to intend to have a baby. It can be an accident. But me? I so wanted you I worked for over a year letting nosey parkers check me out a zillion times, doing all sorts of meetings and forms. They even checked my previous boyfriends out. They interviewed Michael. It was humiliating, but I would have run around the park naked if it meant I could have you, my lovely boy. That's how much you are wanted and don't ever forget that.'

A tiny doubt wiggled its way through my brain. It's still there. Always there. She had wanted me when she couldn't have a baby of her own, but does she regret it now? Have I turned out to be the wrong sort of boy?

Mum told me another time that Michael was adopted, and she never understood why he was so determined to have his own biological children.

I have a question that I want to ask Raffy, but I can't. Not now.

'We'll have to push my bike.'

'Don't be an idiot. It'll be dark and the last train will have gone. It's miles.'

'Can we phone your dad? Ask him to collect us?'

'Even if, even *if* I had any charge left, I wouldn't do that. He'd go insane. He thinks I'm at Felix's all safe and sound. It's only you that's missing, remember?'

'We can ask someone to help us. The next person who comes walking here.'

'And what exactly are you going to ask, eh? "I know you don't know me, but could you go and get a car, a big enough car for my bike, and then take me to the railway station? Pretty please?" That's what you're going to say?'

'My mum'd do it for another child she didn't know. She would. She's kind.'

'Well, your mum might not be a paedo, but how do you know you can trust someone you've never met before? Hasn't your mum drilled it into you not to get into strangers' cars? No, there's nothing we can do except stay the night. Lucky it's not too cold and not raining. If it rains, we can go in that bunker over there.'

Raffy is not going to abandon me then. I daren't mention anything about his bike still being OK in case he changes his mind and cycles off. He's carting the panniers back up the grassy slope and I sigh and follow him, keeping my distance.

'I see you've helped yourself to my clothes. Did you bring the water bottles? No. Thought not. Go and get them and I might let you into a little secret that could just help you survive the night.'

Why am I surprised he's such a mean git? I'm studying his wide, pale face with red marks on from my fingers, as he rips open a packet of crisps and eats the whole lot in front of me.

'Or you could hand me back my clothes you stole before I rip them off you? Your choice.'

Reluctantly I stroll back to the bikes. Stars are beginning to show up in the sky. On the way I make a mini vengeful plan. I twist the bottles out of the holders and dip behind a wall checking no one is around to see me. Raffy's bottle is black plastic. Perfect. I pull the top off and position myself so that I can pee into the bottle. Not much. I don't want it to warm up or taste too strong. I shake it around and replace the lid. I take a big swig from my bottle as I hand his over and watch out of the corner of my eye whilst he gulps a load of pissy water.

'So, what's the survival strategy, Mr Scouting Master?'

Raffy chokes on my watery piss and starts coughing. 'Mr Scouting Master? Is that your best insult? I think the trouble with you, Ches, is you don't have a man about the house. I'd hate to be you.'

'I feel the same. I'd hate to be you. They say bullies are unhappy people.'

'I'm not a bully. I'm not unhappy. Couldn't be better. Got a normal family with a normal mum and dad and a fairly normal sister.'

'Your mum works a lot.'

'So, she's got a big job. Makes a ton of money. I'm going to do that. Make a ton of money.'

'So you can buy friends?'

'A house, moron. And cars, holidays, maybe a swimming pool, a helicopter. Don't tell me you don't want that stuff.'

'Doesn't mean you'll be liked, does it?'

'Who gives a monkey's? I don't see rich people all friendless and lonely, do you?'

'I don't know.'

'Yeh, well, I know.'

I don't say, '*So how many mega-rich people do you know then?*'

I'm thinking about Mum and how hard she works with her gardening and teaching salsa and how she still manages to be my mum.

'What did you mean, "Maybe she wants something more exciting"? What's that meant to mean?'

Raffy tosses me a stuffed black bag with a pull tie. 'A bivvy bag. For sleeping in. Not exactly luxurious bedding, but it'll do. One each. Mr Scouting Master Extraordinaire, me.'

I'm staring at it in my hands, feeling confused.

'If you don't want it, I'll have it back.'

'Did you let my tyre down on purpose? Did you plan for us to stay out? All this time. You knew we were going to stay out.'

He's ignoring me and unfurling his plastic sleeping bag on the grass. Finally, he looks up at my furious face and does his little cough thing. 'Don't be a jerk.'

We must look like two monster-sized plastic slugs lying

next to each other. I think of Inga and Raffy growing inside their mum, squashed in twin sacks, in the dark, for nine whole months. Born on the same day from the same mother. Odd sharing so much from the very beginning. I could have really done with a twin sister or brother, someone to wait with on the doorstep. It would have all been different with two of us. Imagine a mother and father on top of that. Seems greedy to me – so much family.

Everyone admires Inga. I can imagine her being successful at whatever she wants to do. She's basically a smiley person who gets on with what she loves to do and doesn't make a fuss about stuff she's not so keen on. Because she's brilliant at sport she hasn't got time for her annoying brother. Or maybe Inga got into sport because her brother was so mean and nasty. She gets to win lots of cups and medals too.

'Are you jealous of Inga?'

'Why would I be? She's a girl.'

'I mean coz she's obviously good at everything, not just sport.'

'I'll beat her soon enough.'

'Do you like her? You know, as a sister?'

I don't say: 'Do you love her?'

'Sometimes. Mostly not. She's a daddy's girl.'

'Do you think your dad likes her more than you, then?'

'What's this? All this questioning? What about you? Your dad didn't even hang around, nor your mum. Maybe you've got a sister you've never even met. Maybe tons of family out there with no chance to like or not like. What about that then? How does that feel – not knowing? Weird.'

I swallow and notice the hard, cold ground seeping into my bones.

IN A FILM

It's so still and peaceful here with the rhythmic sound of waves and the massive sky above, spotted with zillions of stars. A rainbow haze encircles the full, creamy moon. We're lying flat on our backs watching out for shooting stars. Raffy claims to have seen five already.

'It doesn't look real, does it? It looks like a film set. Like we're in a film. Everything's a bit super-real. The grass lit up by the bright moon. The way all the branches of the little trees are blown away from the sea like they're frozen windswept silhouettes. Loads and loads of stars. These creepy half-demolished war buildings. Do you know what I mean, Raffy?'

He turns over in his crackly plastic bivvy bag to face me. His face looks eerily distorted by shadows and moonlight. 'I do. Let's pretend it's not real.'

My pulse quickens. 'What do you mean?'

'This is the future. We're survivors of a disaster. What disaster do you think?'

I'm not entirely sure I want to go down this route. I don't want to get too spooked out.

'I don't know.'

'OK. It's like this. Britain is completely dark, no electricity, no fuel whatsoever. The few people who live here are savages now. After whatever they can get to survive.'

'So, having loads of money didn't work then?'

'That's where you're wrong. The rich already escaped to another planet with their friend Richard Branson. What's left are the idiots, and they are angry and hungry.'

'You mean like our parents?'

'No, they're the lucky ones who already died, nice and quickly, when the disaster happened. The ones that are left are very fit, like marines, bouncers, gym nuts, but they're not wealthy. They've got weapons.'

'So why did we survive? We should have died like our families.'

'Aha, but we did survive, didn't we?'

Raffy is struggling to come up with a plausible explanation, so I help out. 'Maybe we were in the sea. On a boat.'

'Y-e-e-e-s, or maybe we have superpowers. Maybe, maybe we can fly. That's it, we can fly.'

'Fly?'

'Yes. So, we flew out to sea to escape the disaster and now we have to find food, so we've landed back here.' He shuffles around to find his bottle, sits up, takes a swig and holds it out for me. 'And we've come back for water. Want some?'

Halfway through a gulp, I remember my pee, and spit out again and again, pulling a face and wiping my mouth.

'What's with you?'

I think about telling him, but it's not the time.

'A fly. I swallowed a fly.'

'You should have eaten it. Any protein you can get.

Remember – survival mode from now on. No wasting precious water.'

Raffy is struggling out of his bag.

'Come on. Let's explore. We might be able to kill a goat whilst it's sleeping. There are wild goats on this peninsula. We can skin it, dry the hide for clothing and dry any meat we don't eat in the sun tomorrow.'

'As long as no savages come along and kill us.'

'You're forgetting we can fly.'

'What we going to skin it with? What we going to kill it with?'

Raffy produces a penknife, pulls the blade out and laughs.

'I'm not known as Mr Scouting Master for nothing. This is an antique. Mother of pearl handle, see? It's Dad's. Or rather it *was* Dad's. Only thing left of him now he's dead – in the disaster. Let's get walking. Warm us up a bit.'

We're following the track up the hill where the family with the Labrador and the two women with sticks had walked earlier. Raffy is holding his penknife out like he's expecting to defend himself from savages at any moment. A number of lights shine out from static caravans along the bay, but neither of us point them out to each other.

Everything we've ever known has been destroyed. Civilisation has ended. We're in a different world now – hunting, relying on each other to survive. I can almost smell the goats in the air as I climb uphill and my breathing deepens. I imagine grasping hold of both horns of a medium-sized goat and Raffy plunging his knife deep into the neck. The goat squeals and wriggles, spraying warm, dark blood over us both, but I hold tight and gradually its life drains away and it is still. One glassy eye stares up at me. I can see fear and accusation.

There are a few white blotches ahead. They look like neat boulders scattered about near the cliff edge. Raffy turns to face me, his eyes wide, and he whispers:

'There's our dinner for the week ahead.'

THE EDGE

During the day, at low tide below where the goats are sleeping, climbers scale the cliffs with ropes and harnesses. Now it's high tide and there's only a sliver of beach visible. The waves have washed over where we cycled along earlier this afternoon, where all the cars were parked. This giant finger of land we're on tonight is now surrounded by water either side.

Raffy tiptoes close and mouths in my ear, 'They're all asleep. Let's get the nearest one. You take the horns. No talking from now on.'

I want to say, '*We're not really going to do it, are we?*' But Raffy has placed his fingers over my mouth and I can see the knife blade in his other hand gleaming in the moonlight. He's pointing the blade at a sleeping goat with shaggy white wool and two impressive horns curled like bicycle handlebars. I don't want it to die. I want it to wake up and run away with all the others.

Raffy is uphill from the sleeping creature and closing in whilst waving me on to the other side – the side nearer to the cliff edge leading to the sea below. I am not that idiotic. I won't go below the goat. I plan to approach on the same level as the goat, head on, and see if I can touch its horns before it wakes up. We are very close now. It's hard to breathe quietly. I could dive forwards and touch its horns. Raffy could leap on top of it. We glance at each other and he nods. I put my hands forwards and see them trembling. The goat wakes up and panics as Raffy screams at me, 'Grab it. Grab it.'

My hands close around the horns and my skin stings as the creature writhes. There are loud bleats all around and I am thwacked on the ground. As I try to scramble to my feet, I see white goat bodies scampering away uphill. My feet have lost grip on rubbly ground and I am sliding towards the cliff edge.

I hear a voice: *Fly. Fly.*

But I'm the wrong way around. My belly is scraping along the rock. My fingers are clinging on, grasping what little tussocks of grass there are. And then I am flying. Briefly. Falling. Sliding again until my side whacks against rock, my left foot lodges in a V-shaped crevice and I stop. Gasping for breath. My left shoulder is leaning against a ridge of rock, my right arm clutching hold of what feels like a looped handle. Panting, shaking, but not falling. I can sense the water moving below me, cold and deep. I look up and can't see how I can climb back up. I call out pleadingly like a scared goat, 'Raffy. Help. Raffy. Help me.'

A few small stones tumble down the cliff near my head. I bend my head down, whimpering, 'Don't hurt me. Raffy. I'm here. Help me. Please help me.'

I discover I can get a firm grip by putting my hand right through the looped handle. I guess a climber left it behind. But I can't move my other arm. It's locked in by the weight of my body and I daren't move away to release it unless I can trust the climber's wedged handle. I pull down on the loop with my right hand and it feels firm. I pull a little more and ease my left arm out. My arm feels odd. I want to check it, but I have to keep holding on to the loop. My forearm looks strange in this moonlight. Slightly curved, banana-shaped. And then I think of mango smoothie and start to cry big sobs. I'm howling like an animal, trapped and scared. I begin to hear my name and I'm shouting back, 'I'm here. Raffy. I'm here. I'm stuck.'

'Ches. Ches. I'm here. It's OK, mate. I'll get you out. Remember, I'm Mr Scouting Master. Are you hurt?'

'Yes. My arm. I think it's broken.'

'Are you bleeding?'

'Cuts on my arm. My hands are sore and scraped and my legs.'

'Yeh, I don't mean that, I mean gushing out. Losing blood. Are you losing blood?'

'I don't think so. Hard to tell. But my arm's beginning to throb.'

'You'll be OK if you're not losing blood coz then you'd faint. I've seen it on *Casualty*.'

'I can't see you, Raffy.'

'I'm staying well back and lying down. No point in us both diving over the edge.'

'No. What are we going to do?'

'It's all right, I'm thinking of a plan. Your job is to stay awake and hang on. Can you do that?'

'I don't know. How long for?'

'As long as it takes for me to get back to my bike, cycle to get help and the help get here. Could be a while.'

'Don't leave me. Raffy, don't leave me. I'm tired and I can't hang on. Not on my own.'

'Ches, mate. I've got to get you help.'

'It'll be too late. I don't want to be on my own.'

'What time do you reckon it is now? It could be hours before a dog walker comes. Dawn is what? Four o'clock? No one gets up at four to walk their dog. We don't. Earliest we walk Lupin is 6.30. That's a long wait. You'll get too cold. How are you feeling now?'

'Shaky.'

I wish I'd never agreed to come on this nightmare trip. I should be in my bed. With my mum in the next bedroom.

I start to cry again.

'At least you'll get some sympathy coz of your injuries. Been punished enough. But me? I'm done for. No one's going to be harsh on you... Ches?'

'Yes.'

'I'm sorry.'

'What for?'

'For all this. It's my fault. Bringing you here. Please hang on.'

My arm feels tight and the pain is almost too much to bear. I concentrate on my right hand, wiggling my fingers to keep them from going numb whilst holding firmly on to the loop. I want to shift my body but I daren't. I give each foot in turn time and space to twirl around then lodge it back in the V of the rock. I lick the salty snot from my top lip.

'My dad's going to kill me. I'm going to have to tell him what I saw.'

I ask just to keep him talking, keep him here. 'What did you see?'

'I'm scared, Ches, of losing my dad.'

'Why? Is he ill?'

'No. He's... he's seeing someone. Not my mum. He doesn't love my mum any more. I saw him in the bedroom with someone. Having sex. I'd come home early from school.'

'Oh. That's horrible.' I'm thinking how to comfort him. 'But Raffy, you've got your mum, and your dad still loves you and will do stuff with you.'

'That's not what happens. Dads go off, leaving mums with the kids.'

'Not always.'

'Name me one kid who is with their dad pretty much full-time?'

'Sonia. Jack. There are loads.'

'No, there aren't. And Sonia's mum died. It doesn't count.'

'Your mum loves you.'

'No, she does not. Not properly. We're an inconvenience. Particularly me. Too loud, too untidy, too in the way. She's not going to want us when Dad divorces her. She's not like your mum.'

Yes, he's right. I can see my mum salsa dancing around the kitchen, kid's cookbook in her hand. I can feel her plumping a kiss on my cheek and me turning away and saying, 'M-u-um,' but secretly liking it. We sit next to each other watching *Strictly* or *Doctor Who*, eating satsuma after satsuma. She takes me to Swindon Oasis on the train and even though swimming's not her thing she'll slide down the slides after me and laugh. I know my mum loves me. I know she gets it wrong with buying me the wrong clothes and getting in a tizz over cooking and caring what other people think of her when really, she's brilliant.

'I'm sorry, Raffy. Really, I am.'

There's no answer, but I reckon he's crying.

FLYING

The moon has shifted in the sky a lot since I last looked at it from the bivvy bag. It's enormous and is shimmering light towards me. I'm trying to imagine the sun's warmth shining from Australia onto the moon and bouncing back down towards me in a concentrated way. Like when you get the sun to burn a hole in paper by reflecting the light through a magnifying glass.

My arm is throbbing, pulsing waves of pain throughout my whole body. It isn't a sharp pain as long as I keep my arm perfectly still. But it's an overwhelming pain, making me not sure where my body begins and ends. It's like I've merged into being part of the rockface. Maybe I'm going a bit mad. Or maybe this is what death feels like. Giving up your own body and becoming part of the planet. I don't mind that. It feels comforting.

'Ches. Are you still there? Ches. Please answer me. You must keep talking. Ches, say something. Ches. Ches! You mustn't die. Ches. Oh God, I am so sorry. It doesn't matter about my dad and all that. I don't really care as long as you stay alive. Please. You can have him. You can have my dad. Ch-e-es!'

'Raffy? Raffy? Raffy, I'm still here.'

'Ches. Thank God.'

'Raffy, are you OK? You were crying.'

'Yes. Yes, but I'm OK.'

'I'm very tired and cold.'

'Oh God. Ches, I want to get help, but I don't want to leave you. I don't know what to do. This is really, really bad. Talk to me. Keep you talking. Ches, tell me the names of your family. Go on.'

'Nana Lil. I've got a Nana Lil. She's a photographer. No – she was a photographer. And Aunty Bella.'

'What's she do? Aunty Bella.'

'A stage manager. Drives a lorry. She's stronger than plenty of men. She does boxing. Thai kickboxing. I'm meant to be going with her.'

'Going where?'

'To have a go. See if I like it.'

'You will. I'm sure you will. Then you can beat me up no problem.'

'I don't want to beat you up.'

'Why not? You should. You *did* want to.'

'I don't want to anymore. Raffy… why do you hate me?'

'I don't hate you. I get this monster thing happen and I can't help it. Then I want to hurt you. I don't know. I actually like you. You're cool. Not like me.'

'Raffy?'

'Yes.'

'I don't need your dad. I'm happy without a dad. It's OK. You need him, not me. It's you he loves.'

'Ches… Ches, someone's coming. Hang on in there. It's a torch. *Help, help, help!* We're here.'

I can hear a man's voice. A strong light blinds me, and I jolt, causing a knife of intense pain up my left arm. I scream. I want to nurse my arm, but I have to keep on holding the strap. I'm not sure I can do this much longer. I'm bleating like a lost lamb. Then I hear my name.

'Ches. Hello down there. I'm getting you help – OK? We'll get a helicopter for you. You OK for a little while longer?'

'Yes.'

'Your friend will keep an eye on you for a moment. I'll make the call.'

'Ches, it's me. It's going to be OK. I'm so happy. It's going to be OK. You're going in a helicopter. Brilliant, eh?'

I can hear Raffy, but I can't be bothered to answer. I want him to quieten down. I'm exhausted. The pain is really bad after that jolt. He's going on and on. I'm imagining dropping down, down, down and sinking down, down into the sea, down, down into the sand and my bones disintegrating into sand, my flesh long gone. Comfortable.

'Ches! Listen up. It's Mark here. I want you to remember earlier today. You got your wig stuck in your bike. I ripped it out from your wheel. Remember? Answer me. Ches. Wake up.'

The torch light is blinding me. Stop it. I want to drift. I want to sleep.

'Ches. I want you to hold on tight. Helicopter's on its way. I thought you were a girl. Remember? You're on the news. It clicked. "Ches. Fabulous name for a girl." But you're a boy. Course you are. I cycled out here and when I recognised your bike with hairs in the wheel, I called the police. Not long to wait. Let's sing together. Come on. What shall we sing? Ten green bottles? No, perhaps not. Any ideas?'

I hear Raffy starting to sing, 'Oh, the grand old Duke of York, he had ten thousand men. He marched them up to the top of the hill…'

The Lycra man is singing loudly too, and I start to join in, mouthing the words. I'm thirsty. I desperately want water, even pissy water. I almost smile at that. I wonder if I'll get to tell him.

'Ches, time to learn some new songs. Andy the camel's got ten humps, Andy the camel's got ten humps, Andy the camel's got ten humps, so go Andy go. Dum, dum, dum. Join in, Ches. Come on. Andy the camel's got nine humps…'

I'm doing my best to sing with them. Raffy is bellowing out like a rhinoceros. Lycra man seems to have an endless supply of silly songs. How long can I hold on? This is taking forever. I feel like I want to be sick I'm so tired. I think about sick spewing out all over my front because there's no way I can turn and aim at the sea below.

Then I hear a distant murmuring sound, and everyone stops singing. Tears spring to my eyes. Mum. I'm going to see my mum. I think I might have wet myself a bit, but I don't care at all. Mum. I love you, Mum.

It's so loud and the light is very bright. I can feel a huge draught. The helicopter is massive and lime green. All I want is Mum, but a man is dangling down towards me. Then he's asking me stuff through the deafening rhythmic thwacking sound of the blades.

'Ches, mate. You're safe now. Can you hear me?'

I'm nodding and he's looking me over.

'We've got you. You're not going anywhere now, except with us, back to safety.'

He is unfurling my cold, stiff fingers one by one from the climber's loop of rope. My fingers look like alien claws. It's like they don't belong to me.

'Easy does it. You can relax now.'

I like his purring voice. He's Scottish. He's wearing a helmet and has big arms in bright orange.

'Okeydokey, young man. We're easing you onto this stretcher now. Strapping you on. Nothing for you to do except relax. All taken care of.'

He's tucking a silver blanket around me like I'm a roast chicken. My arm is extremely painful and I'm feeling waves of nausea build through me and sweat sing out through my pores. Tears are drenching my face because very soon I'm going to see my mum. I didn't die. I'm going to live.

In no time, I'm swaying, pulled upwards. I wish I could watch and take it all in, but the light is bright, and I can't prevent my eyes closing. I'm so very drowsy. I imagine I'm going up to heaven… there's nothing for me to do but relax.

QUESTIONS, QUESTIONS, QUESTIONS

I am in the big belly of a huge insect flying in the night. My body is shaking uncontrollably like a crazy pneumatic drill. In a funny way it's quite pleasant. I just let it happen. I can hear a two-way conversation on a radio, but I can't make out what they are saying. I can see a couple of people. The man with the bright orange jacket is watching me and another figure in blue has their back to me, dealing with some equipment.

'Hello there, Ches. How are you feeling?'

'Where… we… going?' I have trouble speaking because I'm shaking so much.

'Hospital. The children's hospital. In Bristol. They'll fix you up.'

It sounds like he's saying, "horse bottle" not "hospital".

'All that way… in helicopter?'

'Yes, indeedy.'

'My mum… at hospital?'

'Aye, she'll be there soon enough.'

'Raffy?'

'He's safe. With the police for a few questions. You were a plucky lad. You held on well. It was hard to uncurl those fingers of yours. Like a metal robot hand – so tight and rigid.'

My brain feels like a swirl of thick vegetable soup. Bite-sized chunks of the day momentarily surface and are lost again. It's hard to sort out what happened. I can't work out if I'm in massive trouble. Is it all my fault for running away? Mum might be really angry, or worse still, disappointed. How can I explain what happened? The letter thing from my birth mum feels unreal, like it happened in another lifetime. Everything feels unreal.

We land in the city like a big duck on water. The loud thwacking sound of the helicopter blades begins to subside. Air rushes in as the helicopter door opens and I am carried outside on the stretcher. Bright lights have obliterated the starry night sky and smudged it into a murky orangey blue.

I wake up. I am suspended and looking down at a gigantic iced wedding cake. Am I flying? I stretch my velvety wings out wide and explore with my huge eyes. There's a strange scent. And a small, bright full moon shape. I try to fly towards the tiny, intensely bright moonlight, but it stays far away no matter how hard I move my wings. Part of me knows I'm not a moth, really. I am looking at a ceiling, a white hospital ceiling with an electric light, and I am looking up from a hospital bed, not down. But it takes a lot of concentration to orientate myself onto my back, on the bed. I mentally check my body. My left arm feels unusual. Heavy. But not painful. More like a big tube of cement that doesn't belong to me.

'Ches? Ches, it's me. Your mum. I'm so happy to see you, lovely one.'

'Mum.'

'I'm here.'

A big lump lodges in my throat. Why does my body do that? Wetness fills my eyes.

'I'm sorry, Mum.'

'I'm sorry too. I love you, Ches, more than you'll ever know.'

'I know.'

I don't ask, '*Why are you sorry?*'

I'm already fading into sleep again.

I awake to hear soft voices discussing something I can't make out. Adult voices whispering about me. I open my eyes and turn to look at them. Two police officers, their liquorice-black uniforms bulked out with equipment, are standing next to Mum.

'Ches, sweet, these police officers just want to have a quick word with you. The doctor says it's all right as long as you are happy. Not long. Just to make sure you're safe.'

'I am safe.'

'I know. But they just want to check that you, you know, *were* safe. I'll let them ask you about it. Is that OK? Are you OK with that? I'll be here if you want me to be. Do you want me here?'

I want to say, '*Mum, it was all my fault.*'

'We'll take over from here, thank you. If you could just sit outside of the room so we can call you if needed. Thank you.'

Everyone watches Mum walk slowly out of the room. She does a little thumbs-up sign and is gone.

'Ches. My name's Helen and this is Steve. Our job is safeguarding, making sure children are safe. We'd like you to tell us what happened from when you left your Aunty Bella's house on Saturday evening. In your own time. In your own words.'

I tell them what happened. I tell them all the events. The places and the people involved. I tell them like I am reading out loud at school, glancing up, wanting them to say, 'Thank you, that's enough.'

But they nod and keep encouraging me to carry on with the story: 'And then what happened?'

I leave out the important bits. How I felt furious, small and humiliated. Scared. In case she, my birth mother – I hate that I don't even know her name – wrote a little, dismissive note telling me she had better things to do than keep me and love me.

I don't tell them about all the confusing feelings I had about Raffy. I had the best fun with him. And the scariest time. I hated him. I felt sorry for him. I nearly died.

'So, what would you say your relationship to Raffy is then? How do you feel about him?'

I redden, worrying that the policewoman might have just read my mind.

'He's my friend. From school. It's not his fault. He wanted to give me a birthday adventure.'

'We've heard that he hasn't always been your friend?'

I don't know what to say. Mum must have talked, or maybe Raffy. I don't know if he is my friend or isn't. I think about him crying and offering me his dad. Singing "The Grand Old Duke of York". I haven't told the police about his nasty pretending-to-drown trick. I can feel his spit dribbling down my neck. Then I remember the pissy water and I can't help smiling.

'Hmm. Anything more to tell us, Ches? Anything you've been keeping back?'

I shake my head.

The policeman squats down near to me. He's got a kind face and short black hair. 'I've got two boys myself. About your age. What were you thinking about, Ches, just then? When you smiled?'

'Nothing.'

Is trying to make someone drink your piss a crime?

'You're not in trouble. But you do need to tell us everything. Anything that might be worrying you. Anything at all. You're not going to shock us. Better out than in.'

'I've told you everything.'

There's a long silence as they both look at me. I can feel my heart thump.

Then they smile and stand up straight. 'Get yourself all mended, and Ches, you were lucky this time. Not to be repeated. You got a lot of people in a big stew about what had happened to you. A lot of people who really care for you. Best to talk to someone if you've got worries. OK?'

My voice has become very small. 'Yes. Thank you. I'm sorry.'

*

We're in Aunty Bella's red Mini driving away from the hospital. All four of us. In front of me I can see Nana Lil's pink dangly earrings swaying each time we take a corner. On my lap my right hand is entwined in Mum's hand. She keeps squeezing it. My left arm is in a lime-green cast and held up in a thin sling. There's a tartan blanket over my shoulders. I've got my own blue trackie bottoms on.

I'm pretty confused about some of what's happened. I

have this strange, mixed-up memory. I know I went in the helicopter, but I also remember feeling like a gigantic moth fluttering up towards the moon, but the higher I went the further the moon was away from me. I don't really know when this happened.

'Mum.'

'It's OK, Ches. You rest now. We'll get you tucked up in bed as soon as we get home.'

'I'm glad we're going home.'

'Yes. You've been on quite an adventure, but you're safe now. Time to go home.'

'My arm. It's fixed.'

'Yes. You remember, Ches? They fixed it all up whilst you were away with the fairies. You were sedated and then had a local anaesthetic. But you're OK. Apart from a few bumps and scrapes, you're OK.'

'I flew. Mum, I flew.'

'I know, sugar. A helicopter rescued you.'

'No, Mum, I really flew. It was easy.'

Nana Lil turns and raises her crazy eyebrows at Mum.

'That was the drugs, special one. The medication.'

My eyes feel tired, so I close them and try to relax as we travel up the M5 towards Cheltenham. Although my arm aches a little bit it is so comforting having it firmly wrapped up in a plaster cast.

Apart from the police no one has mentioned Raffy and I wonder what kind of trouble he is getting into now. I actually want to see him. I know everyone will be dead envious of my helicopter ride and want to quiz me about it. But I want to talk to Raffy about the strange flying experience. Being a moth. I think of the birds trapped in the cage at the beginning of Brean Down. And Raffy's words: '*Maybe we* can *fly.*'

'Raffy. Where's Raffy?'

'There's no need to worry about that boy anymore. You're safe, sweetheart. We can talk about it all when you've properly rested. Now relax. Please. I can't imagine what you've been through.'

It occurs to me that maybe Raffy is in big trouble – with the police. They probably think he abducted me, threatened me with his knife and pushed me over the edge, but the car motion is lulling me to sleep and I can hardly be bothered to think, let alone speak.

COIN TOSS

Nana Lil is patting pillows and propping me up before placing a tray on my lap. 'There we go. A whole tin of beans on toast. I bet you're starving, aren't you? You've slept for hours and hours.'

'Where's Mum?'

'Oh, she had to go and do a bit of work. Good job I'm here. Family's important in a crisis. She can't afford to miss out on the money, and I promised to look after you properly. I've been watching you whilst you were asleep. You're a beautiful boy. Quite exquisite.'

She's looking at me like she's about to draw me. Not gushy like some grandmothers are. More like an artist.

'Nana Lil?'

'Aha?'

'Tell me why there's no photos of your children? Of Mum and Aunty Bella?'

She searches in her skirt pockets, brings out a packet of cigarettes and a lighter, and begins to toy with them without actually lighting one.

'Well, young man, you're certainly direct. Not like your mother. How about this – a story for a story? I'll tell you why, if you tell me why you ran off like that. The truth. Both of us the absolute truth. Agreed?'

Her old, blue eyes are perfectly still under those two big slug eyebrows, and they're boring into me like she can see my thoughts. I'm gazing back at her and my lips draw together into a thin line. I look down and carry on shovelling beans into my mouth.

I speak with my mouth full. 'You first.'

'Not so fast. Finish your food up whilst I have a puff out on your fire escape, then we'll flip a coin.'

The queen stares up at me, indicating that I have lost the toss. What am I supposed to say? It feels a long time ago that I ran out of Aunty Bella's flat. It almost feels irrelevant. I'm fiddling with the duvet cover and hoping Nana Lil will go and make a cup of tea and leave me alone, but she's sitting on my bed and waiting for me to start. I'm not going to say anything because I have no idea what to say.

'Ches, Bella is feeling really bad. She is punishing herself for having mishandled, misjudged how you were feeling about the letter from your birth mother. She was terrified. I've never seen my girl like that before. She was imagining catastrophes and how she couldn't live with that. Bella felt responsible for your mother's pain.

'And your mum, Aggi, was like a rock. Such immense strength and determination – a fierce lioness. She didn't get that from me. Aggi absolutely knew you were out there somewhere, and she did everything she could. She didn't just leave it to the police. She rang up and talked to anyone and everyone. Even that rat Michael. It was she who found out that Raffy wasn't where he was supposed to be. You have no idea how much your mother loves you.'

'I do.'

'Do you? Then why did you not let her know you were safe?'

'I didn't have a phone.'

'That… that is not good, Ches. Not the truth. We're going to tell each other the truth here. Even if it is difficult. I promise I will too. When it's my turn. Why did you run away? What was going on in your head? I know Bella said you wanted to know if anyone had read the letter. What were you thinking?'

It was beginning to come back to me. That feeling that no one should have read the letter because it was mine, but I can't get angry like I had done before. Instead I feel sad. And I don't know why.

'I don't know. It came over me suddenly. Like a big rush of fire. I felt angry… and ashamed. Before I knew it, I had run out.'

'Ashamed about what?'

'All of it. Birthdays. I'm not good enough. To keep. To fight for.'

'Your birth mother, Ches, was a young girl. She fought a big, long, lonely battle to grow you, to protect you. And she did her very best for you by putting you on the doorstep of a good family. You can read it all for yourself. It's a sad and very loving letter.'

My ears were on high alert. I drank in every word she said and replayed it. My heart was thumping.

'How old was she?'

'Sixteen. That's young, Ches. She had a ten-year-old brother, like you are now.'

'What about her parents?'

'She had to run away. She found her way back to England and managed to survive. She was a circus performer. A trapeze artist. She was used to being on the road with the circus so wasn't shy of hard work. Do you want to read the letter for yourself?'

'Why did she have to run away? From the circus?'

'It's not clear, but it's something to do with shame and protecting her family's work in the circus. She said that if she hadn't left, her father would have killed someone or been killed himself. There are a lot of us with stories of shame around our births, Ches. More than we will ever know. It's not good or fair. So many, many girls and women left with impossible choices or no choice at all.'

Nana Lil is turning her flowery lighter over and over in her hand and clutching her cigarettes. I know she is itching to smoke again, but neither of us wants to stop this talk.

'Did she say anything about my father?'

Nana Lil's shoulders rise and fall with a slow sigh and she shakes her head. 'She doesn't. Perhaps she couldn't say. It's a lost story. Also, very, very common. Believe me.'

'Is there anything else in the letter? I will read it one day, but not now. I prefer to hear it from you.'

I'm watching Nana Lil's face and she looks different to me. Not the old, difficult woman with the smoking and drinking and sharp, mean or whining words. She looks softer, serious and lovely to look at. I can imagine her young face. I wonder what impossible choices she had to make.

'Not anything significant. We've no idea where she's from, which country, if she had a country at all. But she did leave you a little trinket.'

'What is it?'

'Your mum can give you that. Aggi might not be best pleased that I've told you all this already, before you're fully recovered, but I'm going home tomorrow and sometimes it's easier to talk with someone other than your own mother. No matter how much mothers love their children they're not always the best person, for talking, like we are now.'

'It's your turn, Nana Lil. Why didn't you take photographs of Aunty Bella and Mum when they were children? You were a photographer.'

'I was. I'm going to get you something to look at and then I'm going to have another little puff before telling you my answer. All right with you?'

I'm hoping it isn't the letter because I'm really not ready to look at it now, but she comes back in with her wallet, opens it and pulls out a photograph.

BROWN BABY

I'm studying the black and white photograph and Nana Lil is outside, probably counting the magpies as she smokes. It's a portrait of a handsome black man leaning against a tree. He has very dark gleaming skin, neat cropped hair and he's looking directly at the camera, beaming at the photographer. He's in a uniform. Who is he? Written in curly writing in ink on the reverse side is "N.W. October 1945, Westonbirt".

'That was my very first photograph. A lovely looker, isn't he?'

'What was his name? NW?'

'Nat Williams. He was my boyfriend, my intended. He was a USA Army Signal Corps cameraman in the war. The Second World War.'

'What's he got to do with you giving up photography?'

'Everything. Everything.'

Nana Lil is sighing a lot and her eyes are seeing things that I have no idea about. It is frustrating. I want to pop into her head and go through it all without having to wait for her to tell me. Maybe in the future we'll be able to do that.

She leans over and catches hold of my hand. 'Ches. I'm getting very old now and I don't know how much longer I'm going to live, what with smoking and drinking myself to death. I want to tell you a secret. My secret. I want it to be useful to someone and I think it just might be useful to you. I'll get myself a coffee first. Do you want anything?'

I know Nana Lil is probably having one of her "fortified coffees" with a glug or two of something strong in it. She thinks none of us notice, but the alcohol pongs on her breath.

'I was determined to be here for your tenth birthday.'

I sniff my hot chocolate in case she fortified my drink by mistake. It smells OK. Nana Lil is back on my bed, sitting bolt upright and cradling her coffee.

'So, the letter from the girl. It opened up sores. Aggi adopting you. I couldn't believe you were a brown-skinned baby boy. The "Brown Baby Problem". There were a couple of thousand, maybe more – "war casualties", they called you.

'He wanted to marry me, Nat, dearest Nat, but the US army refused him permission because he was black and I was white. They called us the "scum of the British Isles" simply for loving a black-skinned American soldier. People judging. So painful. And anyway… my parents were against it too. It was all forbidden. I had to give you away. My mother dealt with everything and I was made to promise to keep it a secret forever. They were frightened that I'd never be able to marry. Have a "normal" family. But I wanted Nat and my brown baby boy. I didn't want their normal family. I never wanted their normal family. I loved Nat, and my baby.'

Nana Lil is properly crying now, black make-up creeping down her cheeks. I hand her a tissue from under my pillow. She's got all confused with me and her baby. I wasn't born in the war. She's crying for *her* baby. And for Nat. For what she lost.

'Nana Lil, your brown baby probably had a good life. He's probably got his own family now. You did grow him. Give him life. That's a big present.'

'I did. It wasn't easy. Hoping, all the time hoping, but knowing deep down that I'd have to say goodbye. It was so soft and plump. That little hand. They let me hold for a few seconds. It wasn't strictly allowed. He took my heart with him. Swept out of the room wrapped in a cotton blanket. Still got a part of my heart, wherever he is. I think of him so often, so very often.'

'What happened to Nat? When you couldn't marry him? Did you keep in touch?'

'My mother stole his address from me and destroyed his letters. She made me feel that our love was dirty and evil. Now I realise she was a very frightened woman who had swallowed all the bad things ignorant people say about others. People can get very small-minded and nasty about anyone who isn't like them. She was foolish and cowardly. Like me in the end.'

'Did you have a choice, though?'

'Oh yes. Yes, I did. I let them bully and frighten me into marrying Dominic. And then that was it. Career over. Dutiful wife and mother to a man I didn't love. I felt a bit like a slave. No money of my own. No love. No choice. No freedom to be me. It was a mixed blessing that he was away a lot. I hated my life. Most of the time.'

'So, I still don't see why you didn't use your camera to take photos of your children? What was stopping you? You could have taken photos of other families too. Earned some money. Like Mum does.'

'I told you. Your mum is a lioness. I was weak. Sorry for myself. I yearned after some impossible dream of becoming a famous photographer exhibiting in America. I dreamt of Nat finding me, but I gave up. I gave in. All or nothing. It's so stupid. And photographs of my two girls always had a big-brother-with-brown-skin-sized hole in them.'

'Nana, when was the last time you took a photograph?'

'Nineteen sixty-two. I'll show it you if you come and visit me. Ha! I've just realised it's actually what you call a selfie. I did it on a tripod with a lead that I had to press to set it off. You see, I was ahead of my time.'

My words are out before I think about it. 'Let's do a selfie now, Nana. With my arm in plaster.'

To my surprise she goes to my mirror, blows her nose, wipes the black-stained tears away and adjusts her hair then comes and sits next to me. I've got my phone ready.

'Can you do it coz your arm's longer? It's better further away. Press the red button.'

We choose the best one, with Nana Lil smiling and me looking a bit goofy. I give her a peck on the cheek. 'Thank you, Nana. For telling me your story. I'm your brown-skinned boy now.'

'You are, Ches. And don't ever think you're not good enough again. None of us are ever good enough in some small-minded people's eyes. But we have to stand tall and know in our hearts that we are, even if we have to make some hard choices sometimes, even if we make some mistakes. And don't give up on yourself like I did.'

I lean in and show Nana Lil our chosen selfie on my phone.

'Huh. Not exactly a competition winner, but I like it. How do you get a copy of this for your wall? Is it even possible?'

'Mum and me'll do it for you. If you'd like a copy?'
'I would like that very much. Very much indeed.'
Nana Lil gives me a squeeze and it feels good.

THE AFTERMATH

Yesterday we had an end-of-term, end-of-year, end-of-primary school party at Raffy and Inga's house. It was only because of Inga that the promised party still went ahead. Raffy had told me at school that he was grounded.

Mum was reluctant to let me go to the party because she's still nervous around Michael Sideburns, especially when Mrs Trunk is around. We had to arrange for Mum to message me when she was parked outside so that she didn't have to face them. She didn't want to be invited in to their lavish, family house. It didn't go according to her plan.

This is how I remember it went.

My mum insists I always thank everybody for everything, so after I say goodbye to my mates, I edge up to Mrs Trunk in the kitchen and mutter, 'Thank you for having me. I'm going home now.'

'Ches. Ches, wait. Michael!'

She encircles me with her arm and holds me firmly to her side, putting aside a large packet of crisps on the work surface. I glance down to check my broken arm is safely out of her grasp. I can smell a pongy perfume of citrus and something sickly sweet. Her long, blonde hair tickles my ear. I look down to hide my reddening face and stare at her bright pink painted toenails poking out of smart, strappy silver sandals. The tops of her feet are spattered with freckles.

I want to go. Mum is waiting, but Michael bustles into the kitchen and clocks the situation. 'How are you getting home, Ches?'

'Mum's waiting outside in the car. I've got to go.'

'Good. We want to have a quick chat with your mum. Coming, Tati?'

Tati? Tati Trunk is her *actual* name?

'Best if you do it, Michael.'

I don't understand the looks between them, but Michael sighs heavily and Mrs Trunk (I can't think of her as Tati) loosens her grip on me. 'Bye, Ches. Stay safe. You're a lucky boy.'

I follow Michael Sideburns out of the house, expecting Mum will be all weird and flustered when she sees her ex is with me.

She's perched on their front wall looking up at the almost-full moon, her back to us.

'Aggi.'

'Michael.'

'We haven't talked. About the boys and their misadventure. Tati and I wanted to say—'

'So where is Tati? Too busy?'

I feel bad for Michael. I don't say, '*I hate it when you do that sharp voice, Mum.*'

'We want to convey how sorry we are about not knowing, not finding out what was going on. We trusted Raffy and he let us down. Thankfully nothing really bad happened. We are very, very sorry for all the worry and upset and Ches's arm.'

Mum is silent. Her lips are drawn in tight and she is staring at the bit of pavement between me and Michael. Her curvy chest is heaving up and down, and I'm wishing she'd not worn a tight, white vest top.

'Well. I guess this might not have happened if you'd got to grips with Raffy's long-term, mean-minded bullying of Ches.'

'Aggi.'

'Michael.'

'Aggi, don't be like this. Please. Ches had already run away. For whatever reason. He was sleeping in our shed. It wasn't all about Raffy or our parenting.'

'What are you trying to say, Michael?'

A hammer is pounding in my head and my chest has a tight iron band around it. I burst out, 'Stop. Please stop. It wasn't Raffy's fault on his own. It wasn't your fault, Mum, or Aunty Bella's or your fault, Michael. Raffy and I both did wrong. It's complicated. I'm sorry we worried you. Please don't shout at each other. And please don't be too cross with Raffy. He's quite scared, really.'

I want to say more, but I don't have the right words. I want to tell Michael about Raffy's fear of a possible divorce and losing his dad and his mum not really liking him or wanting him. I want to tell my mum that Raffy had lots of good in him. Most of all I want to say, '*Please can you be friends and stop blaming everyone else.*'

'Can we go home? I'm feeling really tired and my arm aches.'

Michael throws me a tiny smile and nod and we all say quiet, polite goodbyes. Mum is silent all the way home.

Even though the police and social services had got me to verify Raffy's version of what happened, Mum is still not completely trusting of Raffy. She thinks "that boy is devious". I told her he acted like that coz he was scared of losing his dad to another woman. Mum started flapping about in a cupboard for no apparent reason. Good job I didn't mention the "sex" word, or she might have climbed into the cupboard. She's going to have to get used to me growing up. I've changed since my birthday adventure. Maybe it *was* the making of me.

Nana Lil wants me to go and stay with her in the summer holidays for a while, to give Mum a chance to go to work. Since my birthday, Nana Lil has started clearing up her flat ready for my visit: 'And I don't want to leave a shambles for the girls to deal with when I'm dead and buried.'

Mum hates her talking like that, but Bella says, 'Maybe she's finally thinking of us, or perhaps she just doesn't want us to see the true extent of her drunken lifestyle. Either way it's good news.'

I'm looking forward to spending time with her. We're going to visit a photography gallery for vintage photographs and the National Portrait Gallery. Nana is going to show me her photograph albums and some magazines with her prints in. Ones she got paid for before she got married. I'm going to take loads of photos in London and she can give me some professional tips.

THE LETTER

It's a full moon. The last time I noticed the full moon was on Brean Down, first in our bivvy bags watching out for shooting stars, then when I was hanging on to the cliff edge.

The letter is in my bottom drawer under my socks, waiting for me to read, when I want to. I decided to finish school first and now I think I'm ready. Tonight.

I'm going to sit on the top stair of my fire escape and read it outside. Mum is at a salsa party and Aunty Bella is in the living room doing some work on her laptop. No one knows. It's me, the milky moon and my mother's letter. I switch the light off and let the moonlight flood in. I take a deep breath and do ten touching toes to get myself mentally ready. I undo the drawer and slide the letter out. I'm excited and deeply curious. I take a cushion to sit on and make myself comfortable on the top step, my back leaning against the railings.

The envelope is a soft cream colour and rests on my lap very lightly. If I closed my eyes, I wouldn't know it was there. I read the instructions written on it, many times over. I think about how she might have felt at the time she wrote it, just before she put me on the doorstep.

For my baby boy – ten years from now.
(Please keep it for him. Thank you for taking care of him.)

I turn it over, slip open the envelope and withdraw a couple of sheets of plain paper covered in neat handwriting. It smells of paper, nothing else. I open it carefully and begin to read:

Dear baby boy,

I know you aren't a baby now. You're ten like my brother is, but it's hard to think of you other than the sweetest, softest little soul that ever was. You will always be this way for me because I can't have you growing by my side.

I know you will want to know why. You will think badly of me. Perhaps you will think I can come and claim you back one day when I am older. Or maybe you will think I don't care. Or worse still, that I didn't want to mother you because it was you. This has nothing to do with you. I want you to hear that from me. You are not to blame.

I am sixteen as I write this now. I can't tell you everything because I need to protect some people who I love. My father is fiercely loyal and has a terrible temper and would kill or be killed if he knew who your father was. That would destroy our family. I can't have anyone knowing who I am or where I come from. I can't have anyone come knocking on our door.

I can tell you we live in a caravan. I am a circus girl. I fly through the air. I love it. I feel free and excited and strong and part of something. I want that for you. I hope you find it.

You might think, perhaps she loves her circus life more than she loves me. She could have left the circus and loved me instead. I did leave. I ran away to save you. All through my pregnancy I travelled far away from my family and my circus life. It was hard. I hid a lot. I worked to earn money in ways I am ashamed of. Always I was protecting you. You were a great comfort to me at the hardest of times.

But I had to make a decision. I couldn't take you home. I couldn't look after you on my own with no official papers. I couldn't give birth to you where questions would be asked. I wanted you to be cared for, to be loved and to be safe. To have a chance. I watched out for a good family home to leave you with. A kind family. They may not keep you, but they would see you right. I hoped. I birthed you on my own like many women around the world. You are strong, little boy.

I have enclosed a small charm for you. It's silver and was given to me by your grandfather. It's a moth. He called me his Moth Girl, always reaching for the moon. You are my Moth Boy. Each time I look at the moon I will send you my love and each time you look at the same moon you will receive my love.

My whole body refuses to let you go, but I must. I must. Be loving, be free, excited for life and strong in knowing you are loved by all who have light in their hearts.

Bye bye my pure baby boy. I love you.
Look at the moon.
Look at the moon.
XXXXXXXXXXXXXXXXXXXXXXXXXXXXXX

I'm sitting absolutely still. Transfixed. I read the letter five more times. She's twenty-six years old now. She wanted to keep me.

In the corner of the envelope sits a folded-up piece of thin blue cloth. I pull it out now and finger the soft and delicate fabric. I hold it up to my nose and breathe in. It smells of summer. Maybe it smells of my mother. I cup the cloth in my palm, wanting to treasure this time under the moon with my birth mother. She touched this cloth. There's a faded streak where the sun must have washed out the blueness. It's already half-opened like a flower. In the centre of the blue flower is a shiny silver charm. It's a moth. I am her moth boy.

AUTHOR'S NOTE ON
NANA LIL'S BABY

I n my story, Nana Lil was only sixteen when she snuck into
a dance at the US base, pretending she was older. She fell in
love with Nat, an African American. She only found out she
was pregnant just before Nat was sent back to the USA.

No matter how much in love they were, Nat would
probably not have gained permission from the US army to
marry Lil. In much of the USA at that time black people were
not even allowed to go to the same cinema, schools or even
shops as white people, let alone marry.

When Nat served in the US army during the Second
World War he had to live in a black-only camp. Dance nights
were segregated too but as there were very few black women,
local white women were invited to the dances with the black
servicemen. And many of the women found the black soldiers
to be kind, less full of themselves and great fun to dance with.

About 100,000 black US soldiers were stationed in
Britain during the war. That's a lot considering there were

only about 7,000 black people living in Britain, primarily in the big cities. Most white people wouldn't have even *seen* a black person before.

Nana Lil's parents would also not have agreed to a wedding to Nat, no matter how much Lil wanted to, no matter how good a husband he might have made – purely because of the colour of his skin. Back then, in Britain, you were not allowed to marry without permission from your parents until you were twenty-one.

Many romances occurred and as a result about 2,000 "brown babies" were born. Only one child is known to have been successfully adopted by his father in the US despite many fathers trying. Some children were brought up by their mothers or their families but about half of the children were sent to live in children's homes where if they were "lucky" they'd then be adopted or fostered. They were often the only black person in the neighbourhood and at school. These children suffered awful racism as well as often feeling that they didn't belong and weren't good enough.

Dr Lucy Bland has recorded the stories of some of these children, now in their 70's, and written a book called *Britain's Brown Babies*. In this way their stories will not disappear.

ACKNOWLEDGEMENTS

The Book Guild team have guided me with great care through this new adventure of publishing a book. They have always responded quickly, politely and clearly to my naïve questions and as a result I have felt "held". Really, they are book midwives. I particularly want to say thank you to Jeremy Thompson, managing director for seeing the potential; Rosie Lowe, production controller; Hayley Russell, editorial co-ordinator; Philippa Iliffe, marketing controller and Jack Wedgbury for the cover design.

Enthusiastic and encouraging young readers – Anya, Innes and Ishaan. Older ones too – Jo B, Jane, Alan, Jude, Terry, Jezza, Ruth and Jamila. Thank you. It's quite a thing to put your book out there and ask for feedback.

There are people who will never see this because they have died or don't read or don't speak English who are nevertheless on the thank-you list within my heart. We never know the influence we might have on someone's actions in the future. I have received much kindness and generosity of spirit from you all and as a result have been able to write this book with you in my mind.

And now… drum roll please… a huge thank you to my two biggest fans who believe I can do it, even when I wobble – Finlay, our daughter, and Nicky, my partner. I am very grateful to have him on my team not least for his expertise in clear written communication. Nicky knows this book almost as well as I do. He knows me pretty well too.

ABOUT THE AUTHOR

Clare Hudman has workshopped with school children to create stained glass public art (her work is in Gloucester Royal Hospital, many schools in Gloucestershire, and in Weston-Super-Mare too). She has created exciting theatre for young people, often with Travelling Light Theatre in Bristol. She has appeared on TV as a stilt-walker named Winnie Parsley.

Clare was fostered as a child and has worked in children's homes. Since 2007 she has been a therapist for young people.

Moth Boy emerged from all this experience.

Clare has recently written the prequel to *Moth Boy* where we discover how baby Ches comes to be on the doorstep.

Find out more at: www.hudman.net
Join me on my Facebook page: Clare Hudman @now.writing
Twitter: @ClareHudman
Instagram: hudmanclare